CHERRINGHAM

A COSY MYSTERY SERIES

THE CURSE OF MABB'S FARM

Neil Richards • Matthew Costello

RED DOG
UK

ISBN 978-1-913331-64-1

www.reddogpress.co.uk

Cherringham is a long-running mystery series set in the Cotswolds. The stories are self-contained, though many will enjoy reading them in order of publication:

Murder on Thames
Mystery at the Manor
Murder by Moonlight
Thick as Thieves
Last Train to London
The Curse of Mabb's Farm
The Body in the Lake
Snowblind
Playing Dead
A Deadly Confession
Blade in the Water
Death on a Summer Night

1.

THE CURSE

CHARLIE FOX LOOKED across the valley at the sun, which had now slipped behind the hills.

I should be back at the farm, he thought. *Sipping a nice cold one, Caitlin getting dinner ready.*

But here he was trying to get his damn cows to head home down the hill for milking, instead of stopping every few feet, chomping on grass, then eye-balling Charlie while they chewed the cud.

As if they were saying… *we'll move when we're ready!*

Like everything else on the farm, this herding cows business… all went to crap when Charlie touched it.

He was told a few dairy cows — couldn't be easier! Small herd, low maintenance — big profit, they said.

They eat the damn grass, the machine milks them.

Sure. Right.

Until the damn machine goes on the blink and costs a fortune to be fixed. And what about when the cows don't even want to be milked? What kind of cows don't want to be milked? These Jerseys worth a fortune. Supposed to be made of milk.

And of course, he was now down yet another animal. Had thirty at the beginning of the year, now only twenty-six after this damned TB nonsense.

'Keep an eye on the others,' the vet had said, handing Charlie a whopping bill.

The sun had set now, and the light had faded from the murky autumn sky.

"Come *on!*" he said to the cows.

He had a wooden switch that was supposed to herd them but it seemed he must be doing something wrong because all it ever did was make the cows give him the evil eye.

They weren't bulls. No horns or whatnot. Still, maybe not a good idea to anger an animal that big.

He rubbed his arms at the dropping temperature and, turning to face the farmhouse, thought again about the dinner Caitlin would have ready for him.

Then suddenly, down in the valley, he saw fire.

He froze for a minute, as if what he was looking at was from one of those horror films he loved to watch.

But then — *oh shit* — he bolted, racing down the slippery, muddy slope of the hill, running full pelt to his farm.

Eyes locked on the fire.

It wasn't the farmhouse. Caitlin and Sammy would be okay, thank God.

But his tractor, sitting just outside the barn — covered in flames!

Still not paid for, and now the thing was on fire, its shape lost in the blaze, black smoke swirling.

As he ran, he saw Caitlin race out of the house holding Sammy, his sweet baby boy, looking at the fire.

More damn bad luck! he thought.

Then, eyes on the flaming tractor, his right foot caught an exposed tree root and he tumbled forward, going too fast to stop his fall.

He thumped to the ground hard, a painful landing caught by his right shoulder as he then rolled further down the hill.

Shoulder hurting, he hauled himself up and continued racing, dodging cow pats.

Then, close now, he saw someone running from the right.

Tom. His farm-hand.

Tom.

What the hell was he doing here?

BY THE TIME Charlie reached the tractor, the fire had begun to ebb; the yellow paint now blistered and blackening.

Tom held the fire extinguisher they kept in the barn pointed at the tractor.

But nothing was coming out.

Why is Tom even here?

Charlie yelled. "Turn the damn thing *on*, Tom!"

The farm-hand turned to Charlie, yelling back. "It's stuck, Charlie. These things are supposed to be inspected. You're supposed to make sure they—"

And with Tom berating him — something he did far too easily, Charlie thought — the extinguisher suddenly went on with a loud *whoosh!*

Above that sound, Charlie heard Sammy crying. His baby boy, scared by the shouts, the fire.

He should be inside. Caitlin should take him inside.

Instead Caitlin came closer, her voice just audible above the noise of the crackling fire and the extinguisher foam shooting out, covering the tractor like snow.

"Charlie!"

The baby was still crying.

"Go inside, Caitlin. I'll deal with this."

The fire extinguisher stopped, empty.

But the fire — save on one of the big rear tyres which was now giving off a horrible stink — had also stopped.

The smell — from the extinguisher stuff, from the melted paint, the burning tyre — made Charlie's stomach turn.

But it was over.

"It's the Curse, Charlie. This farm is cursed!"

He looked at his wife, wanting to disagree, to tell her no such thing.

Especially since she had their blue-eyed boy close.

Everything's okay. It's all fine.

But this fire?

He turned to Tom, still standing there, empty extinguisher in his hands.

Charlie had other ideas about how this fire started, and who did it.

2.

TOM

"YOU... *BASTARD!*" CHARLIE said, gesturing wildly to the ruined tractor.

"What? What the hell you talking about, Charlie?"

Charlie stepped closer to Tom.

"You did this. You set my tractor on fire, you—"

"Charlie—" Caitlin moved to stand beside him. Sammy waved a hand towards his father's face as if the little fellow could sense something was wrong.

Tom shook his head. "Charlie, I just put *out* the fire. Went to the barn, got the extinguisher—"

"And what were you doing here anyway?"

Tom had left hours ago, angry, kicking at the dirt when Charlie told him that he'd have to cut back his hours.

Just don't have the money, Tom.

Tom hadn't taken the news too well.

Could he have been angry enough to set the tractor on fire? Charlie was sure he could.

"You left and came back? What, had a few pints and thought you'd show me, yeah?"

"I came back," Tom replied slowly, looking at the three of them standing in front of him, "Because I left some tools here

5

that I need for the weekend. I saw the fire and ran as fast as I could to put it out."

"Sure. *Right*. Maybe that's what you'd like me to believe, you—"

He held his tongue just in time, unwilling to swear in front of Sammy.

"You're saying I *started* the fire then put it out? That makes no sense."

"Oh yes it does."

Charlie thought he had him now. He had read about things like this.

"It's that… that Baron something syndrome. Makes you look like a good guy now, don't it? Tom, the bloody hero!"

"You're losing it," Tom said. Then to Caitlin. "I feel bad for you, Caitlin, having to put up with the likes of him."

That was it.

Charlie took a step, his hand bunching into a fist. But again Caitlin grabbed his arm, stopping him. "Charlie, *please*."

Charlie stopped.

"Know what?" he said. "You're fired. Take whatever's yours, and get the bloody hell off Mabb's Farm."

"Too right, I will," Tom said. "Pretty poor excuse for a farm anyway. You'd need good luck to get anything out of this dump and the only kind of luck you have, Charlie, is the other kind!"

And Tom turned, tossing aside the extinguisher with a noisy rattle, and walked back to his beaten-up car, a Fiesta with peeling paint and missing hubcaps.

As Caitlin and Charlie watched him leave, Charlie wondered about what he had just done.

TOM'S FIESTA SHOT up a spray of mud as he sped down the track that led back to the main road.

"Charlie," Caitlin said. "What are we going to do now?"

Only then did Charlie turn to his wife, worry etched on her pretty face.

"We'll carry on. Just… carry on."

Charlie tried a grin but Caitlin's face remained set.

"But Tom, he knew how to do things. How to work the machines, how to handle the animals."

"I can do things," Charlie said, though he could see from the look in her eyes that his words weren't reassuring.

"I can hire someone else." He carried on. "Someone even better than Tom. There's got to be a ton of people looking for work. Lots. I'll get someone else who—"

"Part-time? At the pittance we can afford? Charlie, I don't know."

Charlie was about to say more reassuring words but stopped. If anything they seemed to have the reverse effect.

"Charlie, it's this place."

That stopped Charlie. He could see the tears forming in his wife's eyes.

"All the bad luck we've had. You've said it yourself… something is wrong here."

Charlie nodded at that.

Because yes, bad things seemed to happen all the time. Rats getting into the seed. Animals going sick. Machines that stopped working for no reason at all.

Lot of bad things.

Mabb's Farm did seem cursed.

"I'll find someone to help, Cait. Tomorrow, first thing. And I'll keep looking till I get help. In the meantime we'll manage. I'll manage."

Caitlin looked around.

"Charlie, where's the herd?"

Bugger! He had left them on the hill, trying to get them to come back down.

But where were they now?

"Bloody—"

Charlie turned into the total darkness and raced back up the hill.

Unable this time to dodge the cow pats, he slipped his way across the field, looking around desperately for his wandering cows, and, as sure as anything… feeling cursed.

3.

A SUNDAY ROAST

SARAH HAD THE radio on loud in the Rav-4, as the giddy weekend BBC host mined the catalogue of eighties and nineties hits, a time of big hair and big dreams, now being played for an audience for whom the hopes and parties had probably ended.

She had the volume up since the car felt far too quiet: Daniel and Chloe were sitting silently in the back, glumly staring out of the window.

Sarah was usually able to deflect most Sunday lunch invites from her parents, but they did have to make an appearance from time to time, and this visit was well overdue.

It wasn't going there that was the problem, it was the fact that every time they did, her parents seemed intent on inviting some random single man from Cherringham or a nearby village, practising their own form of awkward matchmaking.

It could make for some terribly long Sunday lunches.

Though Sarah implored her parents to *please; cease and desist!* they carried on as if she was telling them quite the opposite.

Getting the kids to go was also an issue. They had friends, activities; their lives just didn't stop on Sunday.

It wasn't so bad for Daniel. He was still at the age where he could spend hours looking at her father's massive collection of toy soldiers, all arrayed on life-like landscapes, many painted by her father himself.

Daniel didn't even mind the history lesson that came with examining the grenadiers with the long rifles, or the tiny Moorish invaders with silvery curved swords.

But Chloe?

Nothing much to engage a teenage girl there, though Sarah's parents adored her.

Sarah's mum's one passion was cooking, and though she would try to enlist Chloe's help, Chloe had less than zero interest in the intricacies of preparing a big Sunday lunch.

Now if Jamie Oliver was manning the Aga, that might be a different story.

"Mum," Chloe said, making no show of hiding a tone of petulance, "can you *please* turn that down. What kind of music is it anyway?"

Sarah lowered the volume, opting not to engage Chloe in a debate of David Bowie versus No Direction.

Or was it One Direction?

Funny, how when you become a parent you suddenly fall out of the 'know' so fast, all hipness vanishing at the birth.

"Almost there guys," Sarah said with forced cheer.

She looked in the rear-view mirror but neither child gave a response.

And all Sarah could think was, *Lord — or someone! — give me strength!*

"Sarah!" her mum said, "We'd nearly given up on you. Just about to sit down."

Sarah had, of course, timed her arrival so that they could smoothly segue into the actual dinner *prontissimo*, minimizing the time spent with any male straggler roped into the free meal with an available, if completely unwilling, female.

But when she walked into the dining room — set formally, two tapered candles on the table, the good silverware as usual, with gleaming white plates and carefully folded napkins — she saw that the attendees today were different.

"Sarah, just in time!"

Tony Standish was here, the family's good friend and solicitor, someone who had been of help not just to her parents, but lately to Sarah and Jack with their informal sleuthing.

Sleuthing.

Such an archaic word.

"Tony, so good to see you," she said warmly.

Chloe and Daniel took their places as guided by their grandmother. Such things as place-settings were important for this meal.

But also sitting quietly at the table were the Vicar, Reverend Hewett, and his wife, Emily.

Now *that* was unusual.

Her parents weren't the biggest of church-goers. But they knew that at least a couple of times a year they were expected to extend a lunch invitation to the Vicar and his wife.

More than once, her dad, Michael, had said to her, laughing, "Might as well hedge my bets with Deity, hmm Sarah? You never know!"

However, she had never known the Vicar to come to lunch on a Sunday, of all days. Sarah smiled, and sat down in the middle facing the Vicar and his wife while her father poured the wine.

"Châteauneuf-du-Pape," Michael announced with pride. "Been saving it."

A bit of wine would be nice, Sarah thought.

If she didn't have to drive home. Not only that but she also had an evening of washing and cleaning to endure. She'd been busy at work all week and as usual all her real-life chores had piled up. Sunday in Sarah's house was rarely a day of rest.

Her mother emerged from the ground zero of her kitchen with, not the usual roast beef girded with potatoes and Yorkshire puddings, but something else entirely.

"Mum," Sarah said, "what is *that?*"

It looked like a design for a modernist football stadium, except instead of being covered with shiny, silver sheets of metal, it was covered in crackling.

"Crown Roast of Pork," she said proudly, putting it down, a spaceship landing.

"Really?" Sarah gave her kids a smile as they studied the dubious-looking item.

"Yes! Saw Ramsay do it on the telly, tracked down the recipe, had the butcher cut it properly, then bound it into a circle—"

Her mother would have then continued with every detail of the pork chops' epic journey if she had not been gently stopped.

Which luckily Michael did, raising his glass of wine to the gathered crowd.

"To friends, to family," he said.

"Hear, hear," Tony said.

And everyone clinked, even the kids with their minute amounts, a family tradition that Sarah remembered from when she was a young girl.

And yes — the red wine would indeed be delicious, thought Sarah as she raised her glass of sparkling water and prepared to suffer for the next two hours.

"SO ANYWAY," SAID Daniel, "when the Romans had

chopped all the Druids' heads off, they stuck them on pikes in a big circle on top of the hill to scare off the Ancient Britons. But the Druid leader laid a curse on the Romans, and he turned all the heads to stone and the Romans were scared and that's why they made their town here in Cherringham and not on Mabb's Hill."

"Bravo, Daniel!" said Michael, slapping his grandson on the back. "A fascinating story and beautifully told too. Don't you think, Vicar?"

"Very entertaining."

Sarah assumed that the Vicar was unused to eleven-year-old boys chatting about executions and curses. In fact, she'd noticed that throughout the conversation about the strange goings-on up at Mabb's Farm, he and his wife Emily had said nothing.

Sarah's mum had started it — number one topic on her usual "hottest Cherringham gossip" list.

And to Sarah's surprise — since she had been out of the loop working all week — it seemed that not just the village but every member of her own family had an opinion on "the Curse of Mabb's Farm".

And while everyone had an opinion, there was no argument about the facts. Within the last month alone there'd been two unexplained fires up at Charlie Fox's farm. His cattle had somehow escaped through a supposedly stock-proof fence and trampled a field of wheat. His slurry tank had sprung a leak and polluted a stream that ran down into the river. And Charlie himself had been involved in a punch-up with another farmer at the Ploughman's over an unpaid debt.

All these incidents, combined with a rumour that he'd sacked his only farm-hand, had led the village to the inescapable conclusion that the ancient Curse was doing its evil worst again.

"Anyway — who's to say Daniel's story isn't true?" said Michael, opening another bottle of wine. "The old Roman road runs along the crest of the hills there. And there's plenty of evidence that the Romans faced stiff resistance when they moved into these parts."

"You may be right, Michael," said Tony Standish. "However — excuse me, Vicar — I'm more inclined to believe the witches are behind the Curse."

"Witches?" said Chloe. "You mean we had witches here in Cherringham? Brilliant!"

"I'm not sure witches are 'brilliant', Chloe," said Helen, giving what may have been an embarrassed smile to the Vicar and his wife.

Oops, thought Sarah. *If we offend the Vicar, I'll be the one getting it in the neck from Mum…*

But like Chloe, she couldn't wait to hear more.

"It's a fascinating story," said Tony. "In the seventeenth century, Mabb's Farm was owned and run by three sisters. Run well by all accounts. They took over the farm after the death of their father in the Civil War."

"What kind of magic did they do?" asked Daniel.

Sarah realised that this lunch was far exceeding the expectations of her two children — and she had to admit that even without the red wine, she was enjoying it too.

"Oh, any magic was of a strictly herbal variety, Daniel," said Tony. "According to the records they ran a pretty good sideline in health-cures."

"You mean eye of newt, and rats' tails and stuff?" said Daniel.

"More like valerian and garlic, I expect," said Tony. "Ancient knowledge — actually pretty effective most of the time, I expect. And usually harmless. However — it appears that one day one of their 'clients' died unexpectedly — at which point the village turned on them in a fury and pronounced all three of them to be witches."

"How awful," said Sarah's mother.

"Yes, I rather imagine it was," said Tony. "They were taken away to Oxford, tried, found guilty—"

"And hanged by the neck until they were dead!" said Daniel gleefully.

Now Sarah shot her son a look. He could barely suppress his grin.

"Precisely," said Tony. "But before they died, they said that the fields of Mabb's Hill would — exact words here — 'run with blood and that the fires of Hell would wreak their revenge'. Hence we have the Curse of Mabb's Farm, which seems to be capturing the imagination of the whole of Cherringham this month."

"Awesome," said Chloe.

"Gruesome," said Daniel, grinning.

There was a pause while Helen dished up seconds and Michael poured more wine and passed down Cokes for Daniel and Chloe.

"What do you think, Simon? Can a place be cursed?" said Sarah to the Reverend Hewitt, genuinely interested in what he might have to say.

"We know a place can be blessed," he responded instantly. "Few of us would therefore doubt that places where real evil has been committed can exude an air of evil themselves."

"So you think the Curse could be real?" said Sarah, putting down her knife and fork.

"Never underestimate the power of Darkness," he said seriously.

The table went quiet. Suddenly the light-hearted chatter about Druids and witches had become a discussion about the reality of evil.

"Ooh! I forgot the crackling! Who wants seconds?" said Sarah's mother, instinctively filling the silence in the only way she knew how.

With relief, Sarah saw that everyone suddenly wanted extra crackling in lieu of more banter about the power of Darkness, and in the flurry of plates and demands it seemed that the awkward moment had passed.

But then the Vicar's wife surprised her.

"Simon and I have agreed to differ on this one, Sarah," said Emily Hewitt, seriously. "You see, he believes that prayer is the answer when evil is afoot. I don't disagree. But I also believe one can take physical action too. In fact, I believe that one must."

"I'm sure," said Sarah, not at all sure what the Vicar's wife was getting at.

Emily held Sarah in a long gaze, and Sarah felt that the she was delivering a message directly to her.

But what? And why here, at Sunday lunch of all places? After all, she hardly knew the woman.

She didn't have to wait long to find out.

4.

A SURPRISE INVITATION

AFTER LUNCH THE Vicar left early to prepare for an Evensong service. Sarah dispatched Daniel to her father's study to help him paint a new batch of Napoleonic soldiers, which had just come in the post, and Chloe and Tony went to help Helen with the washing up.

So Sarah found herself alone with Emily in the sitting room.

"Shall we take our coffee into the garden?" said Emily. "It looks like the rain's stopped. Bit of a sailor's coat…"

"Good idea," said Sarah, picking up her cup of coffee.

She opened the French windows and stepped outside. Although it had rained for much of September, the garden still looked pristine. Sarah wondered if she would want to manicure a lawn like her father when she reached his age. It seemed unlikely.

"I hope you don't mind me bringing you out here," said Emily. "It's not too cold, is it?"

"Not at all," said Sarah. "I'm glad to be out of the office. And there's still warmth in the sun. Just about!"

She and Emily walked side-by-side down the wide lawn to the little jetty that jutted out into the Thames. Compared with her own tiny semi-detached house in the middle of an estate built in Cherringham in the sixties, Sarah felt her parents lived in luxury. She'd left home before they'd been so comfortably off so she always felt she was visiting a hotel rather than a family home.

"All this stuff about curses is nonsense, you know," said Emily suddenly, interrupting Sarah's domestic thoughts. "Absolute rubbish."

"Oh, it's just a little bit of fun, don't you think?" said Sarah.

"Not at all," said Emily. "It's dangerous. It allows people to abdicate responsibility. It celebrates victimhood."

Sarah had never imagined that the usually demure Vicar's wife could be so forthright.

"You sound almost personally involved...?" asked Sarah gently, wondering what Emily was going to say next.

The other woman stopped in her tracks and spun to face Sarah.

"Well I am — or at least, I feel I am," she said. "Very involved. Which is why I need to talk to you."

"Me? What can I do?"

"You're good at finding stuff out, Sarah," said Emily. "I've heard that. You and your American friend. And I know you believe in doing the right thing."

"Well, I hope I do. But what are you talking about here? The Curse? The farm?"

"I'm talking about Charlie Fox — or rather, his wife, Caitlin."

"Go on."

"You know they're the couple who live up at the farm, yes? They have a baby, Sammy. Such a precious little boy,"

Sarah nodded. She motioned Emily to a little bench that faced the fast-flowing river, and they both sat with their coffees.

In the distance beyond the far bank, she could see the village of Cherringham.

"Now Caitlin's hardly what I'd call a church regular, but well, little Sammy was christened at St James's last year, and I've tried to keep in touch. Anyway, she came to the rectory yesterday in such a terrible state. Sobbing her eyes out. And all because of this ridiculous 'Curse'."

"Had something else happened?"

"The way she told it, it sounded like some kind of supernatural attack. From where I stand, however, it's just another event in a run of bad luck, which besets that poor family. Now, most of it is no doubt the result of her husband's feeble planning, ignorance, laziness, anger, pride. Most — but not all."

"So what did Caitlin want?"

"She wanted Simon to go to the farm and exorcise it. I mean — exorcism — how ridiculous. 'Like in that film' she said. 'Get rid of the evil spirits that are ruining everything'."

"And what did Simon say?"

"Well, he suggested that the two of them talk about what's been happening at the farm and perhaps pray together. But she didn't fancy that. Not at all. She wanted something quick and more drastic. She said if Simon wasn't going to do it, she knew somebody else who would. We tried to reason with her. But she just upped and left."

Sarah shook her head.

"What did she mean — someone else?"

"To be honest — that's what really worried me. A lot of people in the village have been getting very worked up about this whole Curse thing. But I do believe there are one or two who do very nicely out of a good supernatural scare."

"You mean the New Age lot up at the hippy shop? What's it called?"

"Moonstones," said Emily, almost spitting the name out.

"I'm sure they're harmless, Emily."

"Don't you believe it," said Emily. "That woman Tamara who swans around in there with her Tarot Cards and her Scrying Stones. You know the one I mean?"

Sarah felt that now wasn't the time to admit that when Moonstones opened she'd popped in to try out Tamara's hot-stone massage. Half the price of the spa out at the Country Club and not actually that bad.

"Hmm, yes," she said. "I've seen her around the village. Very flamboyant! For Cherringham, at least."

"Yes! And I'm convinced she's the one who's whipping this whole thing up. At the beginning of the year they were all but going bust. Since this Curse thing took off, that shop bell of hers hasn't stopped ringing. Not to mention the till!"

"So Emily… what if it is?" said Sarah. "Surely the whole thing will blow over — it's just a fad, isn't it?"

Emily put down her coffee cup on the bench.

"Caitlin is a vulnerable young woman, Sarah. Her husband is on the very edge. He's already had one fight. He and Caitlin can't be far from having one themselves. They've had fires break out, animals escape. A farm is a dangerous place at the best of times — when things are going wrong it can be lethal. That little boy of hers is caught in the middle."

"Okay. Do you think that Tamara is using Caitlin for her own ends?"

"*Exactly*," said Emily. "Caitlin is silly and naive — and I think she's easy prey."

"But why are you telling me all this? Why not call the police?"

"Well obviously that was my first suggestion to Caitlin."

"But?"

"Her husband hates the police. I imagine he's been on the wrong side of the law numerous times and the last thing he wants is their help."

"So what about social services?"

"Nothing wrong with them. But once they're involved the whole weight of the state is brought to bear — and the bureaucracy that comes with it. Would you want them looking over your shoulder?"

"Good point."

"You and your American friend, however, are… how can I put it? Independent. Light on your feet. And successful — from what I hear."

Sarah laughed at that. "Thanks, I appreciate the compliment — but I don't really see how we can help."

Emily leaned forward and gently gripped Sarah's arm.

"Isn't it obvious?" she said. "You could find out what's happening up at that farm. Who is causing all this trouble? Who is hiding behind the Curse? Who is responsible for this misery? And — Sarah — I think you simply *must* do it — before somebody gets really hurt, or even killed."

Sarah sat back and stared across the river at the hills in the distance. Mabb's Farm was somewhere up there although she wasn't sure exactly where. Did she want to get involved in this weirdness? Curses? Evil witches? Farm accidents and fires?

"Emily, did my parents know you were going to ask me to do this?"

"Good Lord, no."

"And Caitlin?"

"Of course not. She thinks it's all the work of the Devil."

"I'll have to talk to Jack first," she said, though she wondered whether it would be his cup of tea. *Then again…*

Emily smiled and stood up.

"Wonderful," she said. "Now — it's time I was off. You'll probably want to get started. When do you think you'll solve the case?"

Another laugh.

Solve the case indeed.

What case?

But Sarah realised that whether she liked it or not, she had just been hired — not that there was ever any money in it — to solve the Curse of Mabb's Farm.

5.

WAR GAMES

JACK SQUATTED DOWN at the edge of table and peered across the river and into the distance.

"Recognise the view?" said Sarah.

"Amazing," said Jack. "Hardly anything's changed. Apart from the farm buildings around Ingleston. Otherwise it could almost be Cherringham today."

He stood up and nodded appreciatively. In his youth, he'd dabbled for a while in table-top war-gaming — but nothing on this scale.

In front of him, transformed into hand-made models, spread the familiar landscape of Cherringham, with its rolling hills, its water meadows, the lazy curves of the Thames and the medieval stone bridge.

But this wasn't present-day Cherringham.

This was Cherringham as it had been in the seventeenth century.

"Yes," said the creator of the table who stood next to him. "If you ignore Cromwell's forces camped in the water-meadows. And the Royalist flags up on the crest of the hills. Not all that different…"

Jack looked at Sarah — she was clearly just as impressed.

When she had told him about their 'commission' from the Vicar's wife he'd felt straight away that this might be an opportunity to find out a little more about Cherringham's history, curses and all.

And who better to talk to than her father's friend and local historian Will Goodchild?

Discovering that he was actually in the middle of running a massive English Civil War battle using an accurate model of the area in the 1640s was a real bonus.

"My father said you knew more than anybody about the area," said Sarah.

"Really? Kind of him," said Will, taking off his glasses and wiping them on a little cloth he kept in his jacket pocket. "He's no slouch at the local history either. Still — I'm sure he didn't send you here to pass on his compliments. What exactly are you after?"

Jack realised that the historian's skills didn't stretch to being sociable. So he decided to just jump right in.

"You've heard all this stuff about Mabb's Farm going round the village?"

"Heard it. Hard to avoid it."

"And what do you make of it?"

The historian laughed. "Not much. This country has always been full of superstitions and superstitious people. Nothing new there."

"So," Jack said, "this talk of a Curse?"

"Throughout time, my American friend, people have liked to blame the bad things that happen to them on something, anything — the fates, the gods, the stars, curses—"

"And witches?" Sarah said.

She does like to just jump in there, Jack thought.

"Ah, that story. The 'Three Witches of Mabb's Hill'. Well,

if you were to do the research, you would discover that those three women were really just old spinsters dabbling with herbal remedies whose only bad luck was where they were living."

"On Mabb's Farm?" Jack said.

"Yes, but it's more about where their small farmhouse — at that time it was half the size it is now — was situated. Have you walked up from the farm to the hilltop?"

"Not yet." Jack looked at Sarah. "Is there something we should see there?"

"Oh, I'll say. Amazed it doesn't draw more tourists, though... I imagine to the untrained eye it doesn't look like much."

"What is it?" Sarah asked.

Goodchild smiled.

Guy's a storyteller, Jack thought.

He has us.

"Yes. First, I forget myself. Some tea?"

Always with the tea, Jack thought. Hard to do anything in this country without a cuppa in hand.

And truth be known, he was starting to get used to it.

"Love some," Jack said. Sarah grinned at him. Probably guessing his thoughts.

"Sure," she said.

Goodchild raised a finger, a general about to enter the battlefield of kitchen and kettle. "Be back in a — what do you Yanks say? — a jiffy!"

Jack might have mentioned that "jiffy" had fallen into disuse but their host had already departed.

Jack took a sip of English Breakfast, with a bit of honey, no milk.

Talk about magic power... a cup of tea could feel mighty good.

25

Will Goodchild put his own cup down on a small desk, then turned to his sprawling gaming table with the opposing English forces about to face each other.

"Okay, I even put the site into the model. Used tiny flakes of slate. But," he pointed, "there it is."

Jack leaned close, as did Sarah, seeing nothing but a small rise that led from a farmhouse which nestled in a valley.

"I guess that's Mabb's Farm?" he said.

"As it was in 1640," said Goodchild. "And, as I said, a little smaller."

"I don't see—"

Then, in a clearing atop the wooded hill above the farm, he noticed the small shavings of stone in a circle.

He turned to Goodchild. "Those stones?"

"Yes, those stones are what is called Mabb's Circle."

"And who exactly was Mabb?"

"The old Fairy Queen of mythology. Said to enter people's minds while they were sleeping and make their dreams come true… In fact, in Shakespeare—"

Sarah shot Jack a look; this quick visit to Goodchild seemed ready to turn into a marathon history lesson.

"Be great to hear that sometime, Will," Jack interrupted smoothly. "But these stones are important because?"

"Well, to begin with, they're Neolithic, probably constructed by early Druids for their arcane ceremonies. But exactly by whom, what tribe and for what reason still remains largely a mystery, much like Stonehenge or the Rollright Stones near Chipping Norton. But if there is mystical heart to all the superstition and mumbo jumbo floating around Cherringham, it emanates — if you will — right from there."

"None of which you believe?"

Goodchild laughed. "Good Lord no. In ancient times there

was all sorts of poppycock. Now, the stones are just an amazing artifact. You really should walk up there and see them. There is even the Wicker Man, a more modern addition of course."

"A Wicker Man," Sarah said. "I remember one of my teachers talking to us about that. Something to do with human sacrifice?"

"Absolutely. The originals were often burned in effigy along with whatever lucky person was to be sacrificed. The one on Mabb's Hill popped up some time around the turn of the nineteenth century. More superstition there, if you ask me — I suspect it was installed to placate the Devil and guard the crops."

"And the witches?"

"As I said, just three old sisters — the poor victims of tongue-wagging and accusations. Happened all the time, well into the seventeenth century. The three of them swung by their necks in Oxford. Interestingly, there was quite a hoo-ha about where the bodies ended up. Rather important in those days. No record of their interment — they just... disappeared."

Jack looked at Sarah. He could listen to this guy for hours. But maybe this wasn't Sarah's cup of tea, so to speak. At least they now had some idea of the basis for any 'Curse' in the region.

And it seemed like people still liked to wag their tongues and feed the fires of gossip.

He stood up.

"Will, I have really enjoyed listening to you, and seeing this, thank you."

The historian beamed. "Come anytime."

And Will led Jack and Sarah away from the battlefield, and to the front door.

OUTSIDE, JACK TURNED to Sarah.

For a moment he could imagine the village of some four hundred years ago. The carts, the horses, people bustling about much as today.

But it would have been a time of fear as well, human life so cheap, what with wars and diseases and the daily struggle simply to survive.

No wonder they held onto superstitions. Life and death must have seemed so random and unpredictable.

"Quite an engaging fellow," he said.

"Knows his local history, that's for sure. What do you think — should we go see those stones, then drop in on Charlie and Caitlin Fox?"

Jack squinted against the golden-yellow sun.

"Sure. Be good to see the place linked to the 'Curse'. Then we can try and talk to the farmer."

"Try?"

Jack nodded. "I dunno. Something about this is — well — odd."

"Getting superstitious, are we?"

Another grin. "No. But they could have gone to the police. Instead, it's almost as if they have something to hide."

He watched Sarah's smile fade. "You know I'm getting used to these 'instincts' of yours. Like a sixth sense…"

Jack laughed. "More witchcraft!"

"Seriously. They usually lead to something."

"Chalk it up to experience. Either way, even if it's nothing, I'd love to see a site that dates back to the Neolithic time."

"Which was when?"

"Around 10,000 BC it began — along with farming."

"Jack, you never cease to surprise me."

"And I'm surprised you never went to the stones, even as a kid?"

"My crowd was into different Stones."

Jack laughed. "I bet you were. I'll drive."

They walked over to his Sprite. Standing out amid so many SUVs and compacts, the sports car was a throwback to a different era... of cars, of driving... maybe even — he often thought — of life.

"Can you get us there or should I turn on the nice new GPS lady?"

"Don't worry, Jack. I know how you hate that thing. Turn around, and head west out of the village."

"Hey — you sound just like her..."

Jack pulled out of the space, and did a U-turn, heading away from Goodchild's house and the village.

29

6.

MABB'S CIRCLE

THEY PARKED BESIDE a broken fence that marked one end of the farm's property, on a road that led to Charlie Fox's farm.

From where they stopped, a broad meadow led up to the hill they had just seen on Will Goodchild's battlefield.

The hill was crowned with woodland, just as it had been in the time of Cromwell.

Jack ran his hand over the splintered wooden rails, some broken in half, others missing sections completely.

This was a fence definitely in need of repair.

"Guess Charlie isn't one for maintenance."

Sarah found a spot where the fence consisted of a single rail, and she easily stepped over it. "The stones must be on top of the hill. Can't see them from here."

Jack looked around. "Nice."

Sarah started walking across the meadow, the assorted grasses coming up to her knee. The heavy grass was wet with the rain of the last few weeks.

Jack walked beside her, with his long strides, taking a slower pace. "See — this is something we wouldn't do back home, not anymore."

"Really? A lovely walk in a meadow, why ever not?"

"Lyme disease. Carried by deer ticks. Nasty stuff. Can't go hardly anywhere in the northeast that doesn't have the deer ticks."

"We get them in England too. New Forest, for example. Not so much here. At least I don't think so."

"Probably because you don't have deer wandering around as much as we do."

Jack stopped just as they reached a spot where the meadow turned into a gentle hill.

"You know, this land... This *could* be farmed, right?"

Sarah laughed. "If you're asking me farming questions, you have the wrong girl. But I guess you'd need the right equipment, the workers. Could be just the things that Charlie doesn't have."

Jack nodded then started up the hill.

IN MINUTES THEY reached the crest, where the hilltop flattened. And at that crest, Sarah turned.

To the east, she saw Cherringham, a postcard view from here.

"Beautiful," Jack said. "If I was a painter..."

"Yes. It is, isn't it? And down there you can see the farm at the end of the road."

Sarah pointed to the small farmhouse and barns. A herd of cows stood outside, while a field behind the farmhouse had irregular rows of what looked like wheat.

She turned back to the hill.

A tight bunch of trees blocked the view of any clearing ahead, but she saw a muddy trail leading into it. The wood was made up of tall oaks and birch — a dense dark space.

She shivered.

It seemed ancient. And ominous…

"The stones must be through there."

"Right," Jack said as if he couldn't take his eyes off this bucolic view.

She began to follow the trail, a two-feet wide path of muddy ground that was probably as old as the stones themselves.

IN THE DEEPLY shaded woods, the air turned cold, dark and silent.

Sarah had expected birdsong — but there was nothing.

Finally they emerged from the trees to see the circle of stones.

Sarah's first thought was *why did I never come here as a child?*

She wondered why her father, who loved history, hadn't brought her here.

Although, to be fair, he was more of a museum person, interested in great events, important treaties and documents signed in massive rooms with towering ceilings.

Not really one for hiking.

And she could well imagine how as a child she'd have protested at such a jaunt.

Though she did get dragged to all sorts of local World War Two sites where her dad would become teary-eyed explaining the human story behind each memorial.

That stuck with her.

Now she looked at the stones, a perfect circle twenty, thirty meters in diameter. Dozens of stones marking the shape, most looking like jagged teeth.

Were they merely sitting on the ground, she wondered, or

were they much larger than they looked, buried in the soil itself, their toothed edges pointing up?

Either way — the place had an aura.

"Amazing," Jack said.

"Not exactly Stonehenge, but still pretty amazing that it's here, isn't it?"

"I know. To see something this old still standing… to think of who came here, and what they did…"

She could see that Jack was lost to his reverie, filling in this spot with people, maybe Druid priests, villagers, the unlucky soul selected to be sacrificed.

She didn't know whether it was the wind or the fact that they were on a hill, but she felt a chill again. It wasn't helped by the sun dipping below the trees to the west, throwing this ancient place into shadows.

Jack walked towards the nearest stone, three feet tall. He bent down and touched it.

"Guessing even the lichens on these stones are a thousand years old."

Shows what I don't know, Sarah thought. *Lichens can live that long?*
Then, as if he could guess what she was thinking:

"They do live that long, you know."

He stood up. "There's a plaque of some kind," he said, pointing to a spot at the centre of the circle.

And they walked into the very centre of Mabb's ring of stones.

JACK READ: THOUGH these stones date from the Neolithic era, from approximately 6000 BC, the name 'Mabb's' was applied to them in relatively recently times, circa 1100 AD. The name may have originated in the ancient myth of the Fairy Queen Medb, though some suggest it was named in honour of Lady Mabel Repton in the thirteenth century. The Repton family owned much of what we now know as the village of Cherringham.

Jack laughed. "'*Relatively recently…*' You have to work real hard in this country to be called 'old' I guess."

Sarah skimmed the information on the plaque explaining the history of the stones.

"Look here. Says that the stones most likely served many ceremonial purposes but primarily they must have been a place for human sacrifice, tied to the yearly festivals and times of worship…"

No wonder Dad didn't bring me here. That's scary even now.

She turned to Jack. "Happened right here. On this spot."

Jack looked around. For him, this was maybe a different and unbelievably ancient crime scene.

"You know, with a little bit of imagination you can guess what that looked like. People standing around, watching, waiting for the victim to be sacrificed to whatever pagan god was in fashion."

He kicked at a pile of ashes. "Guess now just kids come up here, light up a joint and relive the good old days."

"Never did that myself but—"

She had turned around, to see off to the side of the circle of stones something looking right at them.

"Jack — look."

"Hmm… what is that?"

The Wicker Man.

They had missed seeing it, hidden by trees until they walked into the centre.

"Now *that's* spooky."

And it was. Created from carefully bent and entwined branches and wood vines, the man was a towering figure with legs, a body of brambles, a grotesque head — and one arm jutting out and pointing right at them.

"I'm beginning to understand why some people think this place is cursed. This spot alone could make anyone superstitious," Sarah said.

"Yup. And we're here in daytime. Imagine if it was night, full moon, wind blowing, and—"

Sarah heard a click from behind.

And then a voice.

"Now you two — you just turn around, nice and slowly."

She caught Jack's sideways glance, a signal she knew by now to mean... *follow my lead on this.*

When they turned, Sarah saw a man pointing a shotgun right at them.

"You two. I saw you walking on my land. Trespassing."

She saw Jack nod. "Charlie Fox?"

The man held the gun steady.

"What if it is? I want you off my land now."

Sarah had a hard time believing that this ancient site was part of Charlie's property. Maybe it was, but people probably had a right to walk on a footpath here.

She thought of saying that they just wanted to see these stones, which might be a lie but it could get Charlie to lower the gun.

But Jack spoke first: "Charlie, we were going to come down and see you."

The man shook his head, the gun wavering as well.

How steady was his trigger finger? Sarah wondered, wishing that the farmer would just lower his weapon.

"See me? What the bloody hell for?"

Now Sarah: "People have heard about the bad things that have happened to you. To the farm. We thought we might help and—"

"Don't need any *help*. I help myself. I take care of my family."

Sarah thought of Emily describing her disturbing chat with Charlie's frightened wife, Caitlin.

"People are talking about a Curse. That you and your wife are scared."

Charlie shook his head violently.

"That damn Curse talk again? Look, I've had enough with you and everyone else. I don't want help, you understand? I didn't need—"

His speech was interrupted by an explosive noise from behind. Sarah felt... heat.

And before she turned around she saw Charlie lower his gun, his eyes wide, mouth agape, looking as if a fiery ghost had reared up from the stones behind them.

JACK SWUNG ROUND in surprise, trying to work out what had happened. But nothing made sense.

The Wicker Man seemed to have spontaneously combusted: every twisted branch was alight and the whole structure roared and crackled with the intense heat. A whoosh of sparks made him back further away.

With an angry yell, Charlie raced past him toward the fire, shotgun waving in one hand.

"For Christ's sake, Charlie," said Jack. "Put the gun down."

Charlie turned, for a moment hearing sense — and placed

the gun against one of the ancient stones. Then he again ran toward the fire, arms stretched out as if in despair.

"What do we do?" he shouted.

"You got any water up here?" said Jack as calmly as he could.

The farmer turned and shook his head in a panic.

"Up here? No!"

"Then I'm sorry, Charlie," said Jack. "But you're just going to have to wait till it burns itself out."

To one side Jack could see Sarah motionless, clearly shocked by the ferocity of the fire. And up ahead, Charlie was now frozen too, panting and staring. While the farmer gaped at the swirling fire, Jack walked behind him, carefully lifted up the shotgun, broke it, and removed the cartridges.

Then, resting it over his arm, he walked slowly around the fire, looking for signs that someone had been up there.

In the woods he saw a flicker of movement. He peered into the darkness beneath the great trees. Was there somebody there now?

The trees came to within a few yards of the burning Wicker Man. Someone could just have set the fire then retreated fast. And the dense forest gave perfect cover.

The fire had started fast, with a *whoomph* of hot air. Jack had seen enough arson to know that natural fires didn't ignite that way.

He turned back to the Wicker Man and scanned the grass around it. There was no sign of matches or gas cans. He couldn't smell petrol — in fact he couldn't smell anything out of the ordinary. But he also knew there were accelerants around that left no odour.

He grabbed a stick that had fallen from the fire, and poked around at the still-burning Wicker Man's base, a pool of black discolouration in the grass…

Then, the top half of the Wicker Man suddenly collapsed inwards, sending out a blast of sparks and heat and smoke. Jack retreated quickly until he was level with Charlie.

"It's the damn Curse," Charlie said, almost to himself.

"Why do you think that, Charlie?" said Jack.

Charlie turned now, his face bitter. Jack could hear the dark anger in his words.

"Why've you lot come up here?" said the farmer. "You and the girl. What are you after? Want my farm do you? Trying to frighten me off?"

"No, Charlie," said Sarah, who Jack now felt at his side. "Like we said, we want to help you."

"Right," said Jack. "We want to find out who's doing this to you. Maybe we can stop them."

"Caitlin says it's the Devil," said Charlie. "You two think you can stop the Devil?"

"I don't believe in the Devil," said Jack.

Nature made fires. People set fires. Or accidents happen.

In Jack's universe, there was no need for any Devil.

Charlie stared at Jack then shook his head. He held out his hand for the shotgun.

"That's my gun," he said. "Don't worry. I won't use it on you. Yet."

Jack handed the gun over, but not the shells.

"Now like I said before — get off my land."

"Come on, Jack," said Sarah, nodding to him to leave.

"Think about accepting our help, Charlie," said Jack.

"No need to!" said Charlie. "I've got your face now — I don't want to see you again anywhere on my property." He gave his unloaded shotgun a shake. "You know I mean that."

Jack looked at Sarah, who shrugged.

Right, Jack thought. *They weren't going to get anywhere here.*
Together they turned and left the clearing.

THEY WALKED IN silence through the dark woods. Jack felt
as if he truly was in a foreign land here, the trees packed so close
together and the whole place so quiet.

What had happened to the wildlife?

When they emerged into the meadow, he was glad to see
that there was still light in the sky. But even in the pale rays of
the setting sun, it felt to Jack as if Mabb's Hill and the stone
circle did indeed cast a spell across the land.

"Wouldn't want to spend too much time in there alone," he
said, as they headed down the muddy track to the car. "Kind
of a strange place."

"Spooky," said Sarah. "I thought it was just me. And with
that fire. I mean, what do you…?"

"Didn't smell anything. No devil I'm guessing. But what
caused it? Beats me." He took a breath. "For now."

When they reached the broken fence at the bottom of the
hill, Jack paused and turned to look back. A whisper of black
smoke could still be seen, spiralling up behind the trees.

"And that is one helluva mixed up guy, really scared," he
said.

"Not someone you want walking round with a shotgun,"
said Sarah.

"I'm not surprised his wife is getting edgy," said Jack.

"Maybe we should try and talk to her."

"Not with Charlie around, that's for sure," said Jack.

"I'll ask around — find out when she comes into the
village," said Sarah. "We ought to get some background on the

farm too."

"Great idea. How about your pal Tony?" said Jack. "You think he'll give us anything off the record?"

"If I ask him nicely," said Sarah. "Plus — there's the heavenly Tamara."

"Tell me more…"

"She's the lady who knows all about the Curse — remember?"

"Oh yeah. The one with the hippy shop."

"Fancy having your chakras checked?" said Sarah.

"She'll have to find them first," said Jack. "Don't use my chakras much these days."

The both laughed at that as they reached Jack's car, and Sarah waited while he unlocked it.

"So — how *do* you think the fire might have started?" Sarah asked as Jack started the engine and turned the car round.

"With a match, I'd guess," said Jack.

"Brilliant. Wotta detective," Sarah said putting on what to her must have sounded like a real New Yawker accent.

"And," Jack said, "we're going to find out who lit it."

He nodded briefly back towards the hill.

"When that fire's died down, I think I might head back up there. Sniff around a bit. Threat from Charlie or not…"

And find out what's really going on here, thought Jack.

7.

A FAMILY AFFAIR

"YOU WENT TO Mabb's Circle?" said Grace, handing Sarah a coffee. "Really? You wouldn't get me up there now, not if you paid me."

Sarah leaned back in her office chair. She was surprised — her assistant Grace was tough as nails and the last person she could imagine would believe in curses or the supernatural.

"I've got to admit," said Sarah, "the whole place did have a bit of a vibe. Especially the woods."

"I bet it did," said Grace. "Though in the old days I don't think we were that bothered."

"By old days," said Sarah, smiling, "I guess you mean when you were at school?"

Grace laughed.

"Long time ago to me," she said. "Anyway, there was a crowd of us used to go up to the stones, chill, play music. You know…"

"I can guess," said Sarah. "In my day, we used to go down to Ingleston church. Sit on graves. Not quite sure why. Maybe something about not being afraid of the Grim Reaper?"

"Whatever gets you out the house," Grace said, laughing.

"So did the farmer never kick you off?" said Sarah.

41

"Nah. In those days? That was old Harry. Wouldn't say 'boo' to a goose."

"Harry?"

"Harry Fox," said Grace. "Charlie Fox's dad. He let the whole top of the hill grow wild, didn't seem to care who used the fields as a short cut."

"What happened to him?"

"Died, I suppose. Shame. He was a nice old bloke."

"So when did Charlie take over the farm?"

"Hmm — I'm not sure," said Grace. "To be honest, I thought his brother had taken it over."

Sarah put her coffee down. This was getting interesting.

"Brother?" she said. "I didn't even know he had a brother."

Grace shrugged.

"Maybe I'm wrong."

"Interesting though. Tell you what, Grace — if you get that quote for the council job done this afternoon maybe see what you can dig out on all the history of Mabb's Farm for me?"

"Sure," said Grace. "I'll fire off a few texts, see who knows what. You guys turning into real Ghostbusters, now then?"

"No such thing as ghosts, Grace."

Grace loomed over Sarah's monitor.

"No such thing as ghosts — but there's no escaping the Curse of Mabb's Farm, roowahhh!"

Sarah handed Grace her empty mug.

"Now put that in the dishwasher and get back to work," she said grinning.

Grace laughed. "You bet boss — but only because I'm taking my own there as well."

And Sarah thought — *time to do a little digging myself…*

TONY STANDISH FINISHED pouring Sarah's tea and put the pot back on the silver tray on his old mahogany desk.

She sat back in the leather armchair and thought how much she loved his office.

It was like time travelling, with its red Persian carpet, dark furniture and tall sash windows looking out onto Cherringham's main square; the room probably hadn't changed since the thirties.

Apart from the slick silver laptop on Tony's desk of course.

Sarah took the pretty little porcelain cup and sipped her tea.

"The Foxes have never been clients of mine," said Tony, stirring sugar into his own cup. "But of course — one gets to know what's what in a village like this."

"Solicitor's privilege," said Sarah. "I hope you don't feel you're betraying any confidences talking to me?"

"Not at all. As far as I know I'm a completely disinterested party."

"So what's the history?" she said. "By which I mean the family stuff, not the Cavaliers and Roundheads and witches."

Tony came round the desk and sat in the matching armchair by the fireplace.

"Well, it's a tangled web," he said. "The Fox family have farmed that land for a couple of hundred years. Few hundred acres. They own the land — they're not tenants. It's not a big farm by modern standards. Has some steep hills of course, which makes life a little difficult. Mixed arable — in the old days I think they used to have pigs, sheep, chickens — whatever."

"But profitable?"

"Well, perhaps marginally — not greatly so, I imagine. But they never sold up. So they must have made a go out of it somehow."

43

"From the sound of it Harry Fox was getting on a bit — did you know him?"

"Harry? Gosh that's going back a bit," said Tony. "He was still around when I first arrived in Cherringham. Real old-time farmer. Sat on a tractor all week in his old suit — put on his best suit on a Sunday for church then the pub. He died, oh about five years ago."

"Then his son took over?"

"That's right," said Tony. "Ray. Bright lad — went to agricultural college. Worked out how to maximise yield, profits, get EU grants and so on."

"From what I hear that's the way you have to be these days."

"Spreadsheets not muck-spreading," said Tony. "Times change, hmm? And according to some of my clients, he was damned good at it. Used to help them out, did Ray, pulled some of them into the twentieth century — if not the twenty-first!"

"So he was popular?"

"Very. Worked night and day to build the farm business. Moved into pedigree dairy — bought a herd of Jerseys. Premium product — small numbers. Very canny."

"They're the brown cows aren't they? I saw some in the meadow there."

The solicitor laughed. "Very good Sarah — maybe we'll make a country girl of you after all?"

"In your dreams Tony," said Sarah, smiling. "Cows come in two colours — black and white or brown. Unless you count 'mottled' as a colour. That's all I need to know and all I want to know, thank you."

"Well in truth that's about the limit of my bovine knowledge too," Tony smiled at her.

"So what happened to Ray?" said Sarah. "How come he's not around?"

"Sad story," said Tony. "He walked out one morning about a year ago. Locked the farm behind him — and never came back."

"Hmm, I think I remember reading about it in the local paper. He just… disappeared, didn't he?"

"That's right," said Tony. "Amazing, really. Word is, the pressure got too much for him. Sixteen-hour days, seven days a week. No social life. No wife, no kids."

"So where is he now?"

"Nobody knows," said Tony. "He talked a lot about selling up — emigrating to Australia. In the end, perhaps he just couldn't wait. Left a brief note, got in his car — and off he went."

"So how come Charlie is running the farm?"

"When it looked like Ray really wasn't coming back — he stepped into the breach."

"And moved in?"

"I don't blame him. He was living in a flat on the estate. One bedroom, bit cramped — and I think he and his wife were planning a family."

"Caitlin."

"That her name?" said Tony. "Never met her."

"So while Ray was running the place, they were doing well. And when Charlie took over, things fell apart a bit — is that right?"

"Ray had the training. I think Charlie drove a fork-lift down at the country store. You can 'do the math', as Jack would say."

"Not quite the same as running a farm."

"Exactly," said Tony. "Must have been quite a learning curve."

"And was there no other family to help out?"

"Just Charlie. He was the older brother in fact."

"What's the legal position then?"

"How do you mean?"

"Well, Ray's not dead, but Charlie's moved in?"

"Ah — I see. Well as far as I know, the farm is still legally Ray's. Charlie's taken on the contracts, the stock, the responsibilities."

There was a tap on the door and Tony's receptionist put her head around.

"Your two p.m. is here."

"Ah — is it that time already?" he said. "Five minutes."

The door gently shut.

Sarah got up and put her cup back on the tray.

"That's been very useful, Tony, thank you."

"Just general knowledge, really," he said. "Glad to be able to help."

"One more thing," she said. "You said Ray was popular. Am I right in thinking Charlie isn't?"

"I couldn't possibly comment on that, Sarah," he said with a wink. "Even with being officially 'disinterested'. But I'm sure there are plenty of people in the village who could."

"Ever the diplomat…"

"Now hang on — you wouldn't want me any other way," he said, deadpan.

"Absolutely."

At the door, Sarah turned.

"And Ray's never been back? Never been in touch with his brother?"

"Not as far as I know."

"Don't you think that's strange?"

Tony shrugged.

"To be perfectly honest, Sarah," he said. "Very little surprises me these days."

"But?"

Sarah watched Tony. She knew he weighed his words carefully.

"I will say this. If you'd spent five tough years building a successful business — would you walk out on it just when you were beginning to reap the benefits?"

He held her gaze until she nodded.

"Give my love to Michael and Helen," he said.

And she left, mulling over his final words.

8.

A WOMAN'S TOUCH

JACK OPENED THE door to Moonstones, the New Age shop, and felt immediately transported in time, back to the West Coast in the seventies and his very brief hippy days.

Actually, it was just that one summer if he was being completely honest.

Ah, youth…

But nothing had changed in all that time: same incense, same overpriced crystals and totems on the shelves — *heck they're even playing the same music.*

Sitar is definitely an acquired taste.

There was nobody behind the counter. Either the owner never had trouble with shoplifters or the shoplifters knew not to risk bad karma by stealing the crystals.

The shop was small and low-ceilinged — much like all the others in this maze of alleyways at the heart of the village — but it was crammed with stock.

Jack slowly made the tour, noting the incense, crystals, geodes, mystical Mexican bags, Indian shawls, dream-catchers, drums, bells of all sizes, meditative CDs, books, jewellery with special 'properties'.

He picked up an alpaca hat and tried it on. One look in the mirror and he took it off again.

On a noticeboard by the door he saw a list of small ads: he quickly took in the range of alternative services being offered in this part of the Cotswolds and started to jot down the number of an organic dog-food supplier.

Just recently he'd been feeling guilty at some of the stuff he'd been giving his Springer Spaniel, Riley, to eat — and Riley certainly didn't seem that enthusiastic about feeding time. Maybe a detox would do him good…

"Anything particular you were looking for?" came a voice from the back of the shop.

'Sing-song' would be the best way to describe it.

Jack would have expected nothing less, assuming this was the proprietor.

He turned. A woman had appeared behind the counter. In her forties, tall, and dressed in bright purple and orange loose silk clothing. She had quite startling blue eyes, highlighted by dark make-up.

"Hi," said Jack, smiling. "Are you Tamara?"

"I am."

"I'm Jack. We spoke on the phone this morning."

"Ah, yes. Nice to meet you, *Jack*. Come through to the treatment rooms."

She turned and headed into the back. Jack followed, not quite sure what he'd let himself in for.

THE "TREATMENT ROOMS" turned out to be a tiny room above the shop, with just enough space for a massage table and a small sofa. While Jack filled out a brief form, Tamara questioned him about his physical health and his 'spiritual' needs.

She ran through the treatments she offered: holistic aromatherapy, Reiki, Balancing, Soul Connection, Tarot…

Jack nodded at each one and tried to look as if he knew what she was talking about. She seemed perplexed when he told her that he already felt pretty centred, what with sitting on the deck of his boat, fishing…

"Not a bad path to inner peace, right?"

Tamara said nothing, obviously not agreeing that such a simple activity could solve one's issues with the universe.

When she asked about spirits — and he made a joke about Martinis — he felt perhaps he'd gone too far. But luckily he realised that the cheap gag had just passed her by completely.

In the end, he settled for a neck and shoulder massage.

Damn, on a case in the old days I could have put this on expenses for sure, he thought.

And pretty soon he was lying on the table with the lights down, the heating up, a burning stick of incense jutting out of the top of a ceramic head of Ganesh, while the indistinguishable CD music — pan-pipes — played on in the background.

JACK HAD TO admit — Tamara gave one helluva good massage.

As she gently kneaded his shoulders, he had to force himself not to drift off to sleep.

And if that happened — and he came away from this with nothing — he knew he'd never hear the end of it from Sarah.

"So, what's with the Tarot stuff then?" he said, his face

resting on the towel, eyes closed. "I mean — you really do connect with the other side?"

"'The 'Other Side'? How... quaint. You sound as if you're not a believer, Jack," said Tamara.

"I guess I'm what you'd call an empiricist," he said. "Gotta see it to believe it."

"That's fair enough," she said, fingers digging in again to his shoulder. "You should join a session. Then you would see it."

"And then I'd believe it?"

"Wouldn't you? The future revealed."

"I dunno. I went through the whole nine yards growing up a Catholic and you know what? I don't recollect one miracle, one vision. Heck, I didn't see many good turns even."

"And what about bad turns?"

"Saw plenty of them," he said.

"Then — you believe in evil?"

"Hmm," he said. "Good point. Maybe I do. Whatever it is that makes people do bad things."

"Well, you're halfway there then. If there's evil, then..."

"How about you? You see much evil here in Cherringham?"

"I do."

Jack laughed. "Then since I'm a relative newcomer, you better tell me where it is so I can avoid it. Unless you're talking about the Ploughman's — evil or not, I'd find it hard not to drop in there on a weekend for a quiet pint."

Jack's humour finally had a deflating effect. Tamara removed her hands as if being repelled. Then, her voice low and deadly serious.

"You wouldn't be joking about it, Jack, if you were on the wrong end of it."

Good, he thought.

It might have taken a bit of push and pull, but he sensed the conversation was finally going where he wanted.

"Sounds like you're talking about something specific now."

Tamara's voice retained its dark tone. "I am. A real evil — here in this very village. Or at least, on the outskirts."

"Love to hear all about it. I'm a captive audience, you know. Maybe you'll convert me."

Tamara turned back to her table of ointments, and Jack could see out of one eye that she was pouring more oil into her palm.

Nice pause, he thought cynically. *Adds to the drama.*

"I take this very seriously, Jack. And — if I share anything — I trust you will too. Because we all must be on our guard."

"Sure — I'm interested. Really."

"Okay," she said, moving round the table and working on his other shoulder. "You've heard of Mabb's Farm?"

"That place? Sure. Some kind of crazy curse? Bad things happening to a young family? In fact I went walking up there just the other day. Up onto the hill."

"Yes! To the Stone Ring itself?"

"Yep, and the woods."

"You felt its power, pulling you then. And you felt the chill — yes?"

"In the woods — yeah, maybe."

Jack restrained his humour. He had the mystic Tamara on a roll.

"Then you felt the power of the spirits that live in that realm."

"Not much sunlight comes through those trees. Maybe—"

"You *know* it's more than that, Jack."

And Jack was inclined to agree, though he didn't say it — the woods *had* felt spooky.

More than he'd expected. And he had seen a lot of spooky in his day. As well as grisly and bloody.

"Those spirits — they're responsible for the Curse?"

"Without a doubt."

"Then tell me about this Curse. It's the actual farm that was cursed?"

"The farm and all its lands," said Tamara.

"Something to do with a bunch of witches…"

"Three witches. Three poor sisters who had the Gift and who paid the ultimate price for it."

"But why did they curse the whole area?"

"To stop anyone farming their place after they were put to death."

"I guess the Curse didn't work then?"

"What? It didn't stop people trying to farm. But the Curse was no less potent for that."

"How so?"

"For hundreds of years all who have worked the land at Mabb's have had to endure unhappiness, death, failed crops, disaster. You like facts, Jack? About the Curse? The history of Mabb's Farm has it all."

"Wow. That's one serious Curse."

"It is enforced by powerful spirits… angry spirits."

Jack turned on his side, trying to gauge whether Tamara believed everything she was saying. Her brilliant blue eyes glowed like cats' eyes in the candlelight.

"And it doesn't matter who lives there — good or evil — the Curse is on them?"

"Exactly. It's simply the way of things."

Good to know how curses work, Jack thought wryly.

"Even the family that's there now, they have to suffer? Even though they have done absolutely nothing to deserve it?"

"That's right! And yes, they are innocent," said Tamara dramatically. "A young couple and a child."

"That's terrible," said Jack, trying to sound as heartfelt as he could. "And not fair. I heard there's been some pretty spooky stuff going down there."

"Fires, animals dying, disease," said Tamara. "Just as I would expect."

"You don't think maybe some local's got it in for them?" said Jack. "You know — trying to squeeze them out for some reason?"

"No," said Tamara emphatically.

"You sound pretty sure."

"There was another… incident there yesterday."

"Go on."

Tamara seemed unsure.

She looked around as if someone might be watching, then lowered her voice to a whisper.

Quite the effective charlatan.

"The mother — Caitlin — came in this morning. She was so distressed, poor soul."

"What happened?"

"She got up early with her husband for the milking. When they reached the shed the herd went crazy, she said. The cows smashed the gates, scattered in the fields."

"Why? What spooked them?"

"The same thing that spooked Caitlin. Across the roof of the shed were footprints. *White* footprints."

"Okay, so some joker climbed up there in boots during the night?"

"The footsteps were not human, Jack. They were made by

cloven hooves."

"Whoa."

For a moment Jack felt as if he was back at St Vinnie's in Flatbush, listening to old red-nosed Father Gately in the pulpit, railing about Satan, all about the Devil's minions, the cloven-footed trickster with all his *pomps*.

Never did find out what a pomp was.

And at thirteen, Jack had begun to look forward to some of those tempting "tricks"…

"I went back straight away with Caitlin to the farm with a few friends of mine who are practised healers."

"That's good you have other people round here who can help," said Jack, sounding as sincere as he could.

"Since the Curse became active again, I have put the word out to all I know who have the Gift."

"Good on you. Neighbour helping neighbour, hmm?" said Jack. "So what happened when you all went back to the farm?"

"That whole place was *filled* with spirit chaos. It was a maelstrom. There were auras, evil shapes. I've never felt anything like it."

"Wow," said Jack, thinking hard. "That pretty much proves it, huh?"

"Mabb's Farm is cursed. It is haunted. There has already been fire. And soon, if nobody acts, there will be blood."

"So that family — what's her name — Caitlin? She should move out, with her baby?"

"Perhaps. But it is possible that the Curse might be lifted."

"Really?" said Jack. "But who could do that? The Church?"

Tamara laughed.

No fan of the Church of England here.

"Not the Church. A trained spirit healer."

"You mean you?"

"If I am strong enough, with enough support… Yes."

"And are you going to do it?"

"If I am asked."

"By Caitlin?"

"Yes."

"Tough call," said Jack. "You think she trusts you?"

"Oh, yes," said Tamara. "We've become so very close over the last month."

I bet you have, thought Jack.

And after all this information, Jack knew better than to ask the cost for such an other-worldly effort.

Plenty, he thought.

For now, he turned back over and let Tamara continue the massage. At least she knew how to do that…

9.

BACK TO BASICS

"THERE YOU GO, Archy," said Sarah. "Let's get you out of this so that we can go and play with the toys!"

Sarah parked the massive baby buggy in the entrance to the Church Hall next to all the others, then reached down to unbuckle her little godson, Archy.

Back in Clapham ten years ago she'd been a regular at the Mother and Toddler Group with Daniel.

God, where has the time gone? she thought. *Is it really ten years?*

Now, she grabbed the bag containing nappies, food and bottles in one hand and slipped Archy out of his warm outdoor onesie with the other — all the while pushing the buggy out of the way with her foot. It felt as though nothing had changed.

She rarely got a chance to take Archy out on her own — so this was a great excuse. Archy's mum Lucy was Grace's older sister — and Sarah had been really overwhelmed to be asked to be his godmother last year.

Sarah was fond of both sisters. Of all the new friends she'd made since returning to Cherringham these were the most like-minded.

Also the most understanding.

The moment she'd heard that Caitlin Fox came every week

to the mums' get together, she'd given Lucy a ring and asked for her help. She'd been quite up front: "This is the only way I'm going to get to chat to Caitlin — and it'll give you a morning off at the same time."

Lucy had laughed and said for a small fee Sarah could have Archy every Tuesday morning if she really wanted...

So here she was — proxy mother of a one-year-old. And, in truth, loving every single minute of hugging Archy and playing with him.

With the baby in her arms, she opened the main door to the Church Hall and went in. The noise was familiar and welcoming.

Fifteen or so mums and a few dads were sitting on the floor or grabbing coffee and little cups of squash from a serving hatch. Plastic chairs were scattered all around.

Among the parents on rugs and cushions, were around twenty babies, some lying, some crawling and a few just tottering around ready to topple over. Toys were scattered everywhere.

The conversation was warm, animated and relaxed and Sarah felt a sudden deep longing for these days again. No matter that they were exhausting, stressful, never-ending — they were also so intense and life-affirming.

Life on the planet made total sense.

And looking at the other parents she was suddenly reminded of the friends she'd left behind in London, when her life there had fallen apart.

Archy suddenly attempted to leap from her arms and she managed to grab hold of him just before he tumbled to the wooden floor.

Phew — concentrate girl, remember you're a mum again.

She carried him over to a small group sitting on the floor

and plonked him down — within seconds he'd grabbed a toy and was chewing on it.

"Hello, Archy!" said a woman next to her. "You swapped Lucy for a new model then?" She smiled at Sarah before introducing herself and the little girl at her feet.

"I'm Ali, and this is Mira."

"Hi — I'm Sarah. Archy's godmother. Lucy's getting the morning off."

"Lucky her — don't suppose you fancy Mira for a day, do you?" asked Ali, with a grin.

"Tempting. But they're quite a handful, aren't they? I've done my time," said Sarah. "Got teenagers now — that's a whole different set of problems."

Archy started crawling towards the door so Sarah got up and fetched him back. She'd forgotten how these conversations were ruled by the random movements of the children.

"Anyone you know here?" said Ali, gesturing round at the other parents.

"Well, actually, there are some familiar faces,"

"Let's go grab a coffee and I'll introduce you. It's a fair old mix."

"That's the nice thing about being in a village," said Sarah. "Back in London, these things could turn snobbish."

"Oh you won't completely escape that," said Ali. "Only difference is, a village this size, there's no choice but to muck in together. Come on."

And with that, Ali led her through the crawling babies to the coffee hatch.

IT TOOK SARAH half an hour to work her way innocently

round the group — which expanded as the morning wore on — but eventually she found a space in a corner next to the woman who Ali had told her was Caitlin Fox.

Caitlin looked as Irish as her name suggested — red hair, green eyes. She also looked like someone who was made to laugh and have fun — but here, sitting on a corner of a blanket on the ground, she looked pale and tired.

Sarah sat beside her, with Archy on her lap.

"Hi there," she said. "I'm Sarah. And this is my godson, Archy. And who've we got here?"

Caitlin turned slowly to look at her, then back at the red-headed little boy who was pushing a car back and forth on the rug in front of her.

God, she looks all in, thought Sarah.

"This is Sammy," she said.

"Ah so you must be Caitlin?" said Sarah, now feeling uncomfortable at the way she'd set this up.

Was it deceitful? She wasn't actually lying — Archy was her godson, after all. But she was using him — and Lucy — to get information. She pushed the thoughts away.

This was in Caitlin's interest.

The bedraggled mother nodded at Sarah, but said nothing.

"Play nicely now, Sammy," she said, as her little boy grabbed at a toy.

"Pretty exhausting, aren't they?" said Sarah. "I'm just so lucky I don't have to do this every day. You getting much sleep yet?"

Caitlin looked right at Sarah for a moment.

Almost… as if she could see right through her.

Talk about a chill.

"Don't you mean — what's it like living under a curse?" said Caitlin, her voice brittle. "You don't have to pretend you don't know. It's all anybody wants to talk about."

"I'm sorry," said Sarah. "I–I just didn't want to bring it up."

"And you know what? I don't mind talking about it. I'm happy to talk about it. In fact, some days I think it's all I do talk about. The bloody farm. That—" she lowered her voice, "—damned Curse."

"It must be difficult," said Sarah.

"Difficult? That's an understatement."

Sarah was aware of one or two of the other mums looking over, hushed voices, comments…

"Are you getting any help?" she said.

"What help is there?" said Caitlin. "We're stuck there. Can't leave. Can't stay. Trapped."

"But can't you just go back to where you used to live? Give up the farm?"

"Back to the old flat? I'd do it like a shot."

"So why don't you?"

"Charlie — my husband — he won't leave."

"But if you're not happy there?"

"We're *miserable* there. And that's the truth. Not like it used to be."

"When you lived in the flat, you mean?"

"Before we moved to that bloody farm we were happy. Charlie was happy. It was no bigger than a shoebox, that place, and we had no money. But we were happy."

"But not since you came to the farm?"

The question seemed to give Caitlin pause. Sarah felt that under those sad, tired eyes there was a very shrewd and aware young woman.

"It was like… Charlie went all cold on me. He wasn't the same man I married anymore. And then those things began happening."

"What things?"

"All the bad things. The scary things,"

"You mean the Curse?"

"Those witches live, that's what everyone says. And they're punishing us just because we're there."

"Things like what?"

"Like fires just starting. Spooking and hurting the animals. They're making Charlie go mad — and me too."

Sarah was aware that around them, the other parents had cleared away. She and Caitlin were almost on their own now in the corner of the room, with the two little boys playing on the rug in front of them.

"And you're sure there's not an explanation for it all?" said Sarah. "Maybe someone's got a grudge. Wants you off the property?"

Caitlin turned and faced Sarah, her face set, and whispered: "It isn't people doing this. I've seen the Devil's own footsteps on the roof! And I got friends, people who know about these things, who say the Devil is there on the farm."

"What people?"

"People with the Gift. People who can see the Devil. And they say he's there all right: in the fields, in the barns, in the house," she paused. "In the *bedrooms*."

"You can't be sure, Caitlin."

"Oh, but I am. It's the witches, see? They don't want us on Mabb's Farm. We should never have moved in. And they won't be happy till we're gone."

Sarah realised the room was silent. All the parents had gone.

It was as if a wave had broken, sending kids, toys, mothers and fathers scattering away from a stormy shore.

There was just one little old lady in the kitchen. She was drying the coffee cups with a cloth, and watching them through the serving hatch.

Sarah picked up Archy and stood.

"Time for me to go, Caitlin," she said. "I'd like to help you. Maybe I could?"

"We don't need help. We just need to leave."

The whisper had vanished.

There could be no doubt about what Caitlin wanted to do. Sarah nodded, accepting. Then a small smile.

"I'll give you a hand with your stuff."

And she helped Caitlin pack up.

IT TOOK A few minutes to put everything in the buggies and then together they walked down the path which ran alongside the church and down towards the High Street.

Sarah looked up. From here, through the trees, she could just see the little window at the back of her office. She really needed to take Archy home, and get back to work.

"Are you parked in the square?" she asked Caitlin.

"No," said Caitlin. "Charlie's picking me up. In fact — there he is."

She pointed to the church gate — and Sarah's heart plummeted.

There, leaning against a Ford pick-up, arms folded — was Charlie Fox.

It was too late to turn away. Charlie had already seen her. She'd have to brazen it out.

"Sorry Charlie, we were chatting and I just didn't see the time," said Caitlin as they approached.

"Chatting were you?" he said, stepping forward and standing face to face with Sarah. "I bet you were."

Sarah spun the buggy round so Archy wouldn't see this, and stood her ground. Charlie was angry — and frightening. But she knew he wouldn't do anything here, right in the heart of the village — and not with children here too.

"Get Sammy in," he ordered.

"What's the matter, love?" said Caitlin, confused by Charlie's anger — directed not at her, but at Sarah.

"Just put the damn buggy in the back and get him in — didn't you hear me, woman?"

While Caitlin went round the pickup with her son and dealt with the buggy, Charlie leaned even further into Sarah's face.

"I don't know what your game is, but you stay away from my family — you hear?"

Sarah was glad she had Archy as a plausible prop. And Charlie didn't have a shotgun.

"Mr Fox, Caitlin and I were just—"

"I warned you once. Now hear this — if I see you anywhere near us again — anywhere near my farm, my wife, my son — I swear I'll…"

He hesitated, the word 'kill' seemingly on his lips.

"—do something. I swear to God."

"Charlie, what's—"

"Get in the car," he said over his shoulder.

Sarah stood motionless, her body between the buggy and Charlie.

Then she watched Charlie, certainly not happy, turn and climb into the pickup and, with a roar of the engine, drive off.

Sarah instantly spun the buggy round to check on Archy.

He was fast asleep and hadn't noticed a thing.

Babies…

Sarah let out a breath and realised she was shaking.

Was Charlie's threat real? She felt out of her depth and

wished Jack had been there.

Because — in her own village square — she felt scared.

10.

HAPPY HOUR AT THE PLOUGHMAN'S

JACK SMILED AT the barmaid, Ellie, and took his pint of Wadworth's. Didn't seem quite right to hit the pub after such a mystical experience with the mysterious and — ultimately — helpful Tamara.

But he felt that if people were talking about Charlie and the Curse, then the Ploughman's might be rumour-central.

He turned around. After months of feeling like he stood out as if he had walked off a spaceship from Planet USA, no one now seemed to take any note.

Could it be he was now accepted as a pub regular? Still a 'Yank' but able to stand at the bar, sip his beer, chat if he wanted to, or not, and just enjoy the moment?

If so, then that felt damn good. He had known that making a second home — especially after an amazing loss, after a full life — wouldn't be easy.

But somehow, he might be, slowly, steadily, doing just that.

Ellie said, "Expecting anyone, Jack?"

Jack turned back to the barmaid. "Nope. Just enjoying my beer, Ellie. Though I might stick for a bite. Anything good on the menu tonight?"

"Got the chef's special meatloaf — least, he calls it 'special'.

Just tastes like the same old, same old, if you know what I mean."

"Not much harm you can do to a meatloaf," Jack said, and she laughed.

Jack turned away, taking in the room. If he was looking for people chattering, he'd found them.

The table in the corner was usually occupied by a random assortment of local farmers, and tonight was no exception.

Jack took his beer and sailed on over.

Thinking: *Let's see just how much of a regular I really am...*

"MIND IF I join you?"

Jack looked at the three men at the table. He knew Pete Butterworth already from when he and Sarah had helped the man recover a valuable Roman plate that had gone missing.

"Jack, sure. Know this lot?"

Jack pulled over a wooden chair from a nearby table. He could tell the other men were eyeing him a bit. Which made sense. By now, the fact that Jack got involved in local matters — missing items, missing people — was well known.

And who didn't have secrets that they'd rather keep just that — secret?

"Tom Hodge, Phil Nailor," Pete said making introductions. The two men nodded.

Neither seemed delighted at the new person at the table.

Jack nodded back.

Tom Hodge. The man who Charlie had fired.

Pay dirt, as they say.

He knew he had interrupted whatever they were talking about — another odd sign. Being fired, Tom must have a big grudge. Pete might also know things, be able to help, though the club of farmers was probably tightly knit and protective.

"Helluva thing, hmm?" Jack said.

Always good to lob out something that has people wondering... *what are you talking about?*

Pete took the bait. "What's that then, Jack?"

"The troubles on Mabb's Farm, all that talk of a curse. Something going on?"

And that was all Tom Hodge needed to hear.

"Too right something's going on. That Charlie is daft. A nutter when it comes to running a farm. I'm amazed he doesn't try to milk them cows from their ears."

The men laughed, and Jack joined in, taking a big sip of beer.

"No talent for farming, eh?"

"Talent?" Tom snorted. "The man shouldn't be allowed anywhere *near* a farm."

"A real screw-up," Phil Nailor added.

Jack turned to look at Phil.

Amazing how much people want to talk about things, Jack thought.

Especially when they had a beef with someone. Tom had one for sure. Did Phil, too?

"Come on, Phil," Pete said. "That was an accident, could've—"

Phil turned to Pete. "Charlie and me went fifty-fifty on that damn spreader, and when I got it back, the thing was a wreck. Couldn't operate the bloody machine, money down the drain!"

Tom laughed. "Guess no one told Charlie that you had to put some oil in it."

More laughter, but Phil still glowered, clearly not in a forgiving mood.

"A write-off, huh?" Jack said.

"Too bloody right. So my machine and my money, are gone!"

Jack nodded. Two men here, both with no love for Charlie Fox.

He turned to Pete. At least he didn't seem to have an axe to grind.

"So tell me — if Charlie is so bad at farming, what's he doing with a farm?"

"Good question that, Jack. Bit of a story too. You see, his dad—"

"Harry?" Jack said.

A pause there, perhaps as they realised that Jack wasn't simply idly interested in the events on the farm.

"Yup. Right. Harry. In his will, he left the property, the farmhouse, left it all to Ray—"

"Now *there* was someone who knew farming," Tom pronounced.

"Nothing for Charlie?"

"I guess," Pete continued, "that his dad could see that Charlie didn't have it in him."

"Unlucky Charlie is what we call him!"

"Ray did well?"

"Sure, good crops, excellent dairyman. Place ran like a clock. Right, Tom? You worked with Ray before Charlie took over, didn't you?"

Another pause.

Interesting…

Then: "Yep. Place hummed, it did. And as soon as Ray left, it started going straight down the tubes."

Jack looked around at the three of them. "And Ray?"

"Left a note," Pete said. "A bit about 'time to move on'… so he did."

"Police weren't curious?"

Pete shook his head. "No sign of foul play. Man's free to do what he wanted. There were rumours of a woman somewhere, Australia I think. And the note said that Charlie could keep an eye on the place until - or if - he came back."

"Strange," Jack said.

"Why's that?" Pete said.

"Ray must have known Charlie would screw it all up. And yet—"

Jack paused. The men had nothing to say about that.

And that's because, Jack thought, *it is strange. Foul play or no foul play, there's something odd there.*

"And the Curse?" Jack asked.

"If stupidity is a curse," Phil said.

But Tom nodded. "Tell you what though, there's something not right about that place, that's for sure. Always got a bad feeling, especially when I was on the hill, away from the farmhouse. You could feel it."

Score another believer for Team Curse, Jack thought.

"All bollocks to me," Pete said. "Man simply shouldn't be running a farm."

Jack noticed that with more questions, more chatter about Charlie - Phil Nailor had grown quiet.

Could be something.

Or not.

Jack was about to order another beer, maybe a round for very helpful table.

When his phone buzzed.

Sarah.

"Hi, glad you called, I was thinking—"

But Sarah's voice on the other end stopped him cold.

"Jack — something's happened."

"The kids, you… all right?"

"Yes." The shrill tone hadn't faded. "But can you come to my place quickly? You've got to see this…"

"Be right there."

Jack looked at the men.

"Gotta run. Thanks for the company."

And the men nodded as Jack raced out of The Ploughman's.

11.

A DIRE WARNING

SARAH WAS AT the door waiting for Jack.

She looked scared, her voice hushed.

"Thanks for coming so soon. Kids haven't seen it. Has me spooked, I tell you—"

"Hang on — what does?"

Sarah looked left and right, as if checking whether Chloe or Daniel were within earshot.

"Come and see…"

She led Jack to the back door that opened onto the small garden.

"It's weird, Jack," Sarah said before pushing open the door.

AT FIRST, ALL Jack could tell was that the rain seemed to be going sideways. It had turned that nasty. Worse, a steady breeze was making the bushes and trees bend one way, then the other before — in a sudden lull — snapping back into place.

Like hurricane weather, Jack thought.

And yet we're not exactly on the tip of Cape Cod.

Both he and Sarah now getting splattered by the rain.

"Want me to get you a waterproof?"

Jack shook his head.

"What am I looking at?"

Again Sarah looked away, checking on the children. Whatever it was, it was something she didn't want them seeing.

Then she just pointed. "That!"

And Jack looked out to the garden, only scant light from the kitchen windows, then... he spotted something standing in the middle of the grass.

At first it was hard to say what it could be. But then—

"It's—"

He turned to Sarah.

She finished his sentence.

"It's part of the Wicker Man. Right. A charred arm, looks like, with that claw-like hand. Stuck in the ground."

"God. Someone put it there."

"*The Curse...*" Sarah said, a half-hearted attempt at humour.

Jack quickly turned to her to make sure she didn't mean to be taken seriously. An uneasy smile confirmed that fact.

Still...

"Why would someone stick that in my garden?" she asked.

Jack shook his head. He had grown fond of Sarah, really fond of her, her kids.

And he didn't like this at all.

"I don't know," he said.

He didn't want to make her any more concerned, but right now he was most definitely alarmed.

"Jack, there's something else. I haven't gone out there. But it's holding something in its hand. I can't make it out. But there's definitely something."

Impossible to see from here. A lump, something dark clutched in the burned-black wicker hand.

"Only one way to find out," he said. "Got a couple of brollies?"

Sarah nodded, and walked back into the house, while Jack shut the door and waited, thinking, worrying.

STEPPING OUTSIDE, the wind began ripping at the umbrellas. Even with the dome of each umbrella facing directly into the wind, it seemed like the struts would soon give way.

"Nasty night," he said.

Pointing out the obvious.

They got soaked even as they walked the few steps to the stump of the Wicker Man.

A quick look, then inside, Jack thought.

A line reverberated.

'*It ain't a fit night out for man or beast.*'

As they reached the arm, that line seemed more than apt.

Sarah remained standing, letting Jack bend over to look at the thing in the Wicker Man's brambly hand.

"It's a bird,' Jack said. "Hard to say what it is, it's small though, a raven maybe? Or one of those magpies." He took a breath, knowing that both of them had to be thinking the same thing.

Who had put the arm there, and who had gone to the trouble of placing a dead bird in its grasp?

Creepy didn't quite capture it.

"Let's go back inside," Sarah said over the rat-a-tat of the rain on the umbrellas.

THEY SAT AT the kitchen table. Sarah had grabbed two towels

so they could dry off. Daniel and Chloe surfaced but they were used to Mum and her detective friend, so no awkward questions were asked.

Later Sarah would go out, when the rain eased, dispose of the thing.

She had brought out a half-full bottle of Glenmorangie, and two tumblers.

"Ice?" she said, "Water? Sorry, I don't have the ingredients for a martini. Promise to rectify that."

Jack smiled as she poured him a couple of fingers. Having him here made things feel a lot better, though she was still rattled: someone had invaded her space and marked it with a sinister message.

"Hey, I'd have to be some kind of idiot to complain about a drop of one very fine single-malt. This — neat — will do fine."

She smiled and poured herself half as much.

"So what do you make of that?"

She knew him well enough by now to know that, when he was quiet, it was because he was mulling things over. He still radiated strength and concern, but he was silent, like he'd gone somewhere dark and deep.

He took another sip.

"Guess you'd have to say, it's a kind of warning."

"To me? Why warn me? What have I done?"

Jack smiled as if he had heard similar protestations before — which she knew he most certainly had.

"Okay, look at it this way, Sarah. We know that there is no Curse. Someone is terrifying that poor couple, for reasons unknown, and now you're trying to help them work out what's going on."

Sarah nodded.

"In fact, I probably have the other arm waiting on my boat

somewhere. Though Riley would do a good job of chasing off anyone with that idea. Reminds me — *you* should get a dog."

"That's exactly what the kids say. I've got enough to do, thank you very much."

He grinned at that. "Man and woman's best friend. And if you plan on sticking with our amateur detective work, it could be useful to have one. Nothing like loud barks from a really large dog to scare people away."

"I'll consider it. So that out there, it's a warning? And the bird?"

"I was hoping you could tell me that. Does it have some significance, a dead raven, the Wicker Man... or is it just more mixed up mumbo-jumbo?"

"I don't know but either way, the message is clear."

"I agree. 'Stay out of this.' Which, I can guess—"

"—I'm not going to do."

"Now how did I know that's exactly what you'd say?"

He told her about his pub chat and she described her not-too-friendly encounter with Charlie.

"Maybe this means we're onto something?"

"Not sure about that. We have Tamara testifying to the work of evil forces, and of course Tom Hodge and Phil Nailor both would have it in for Charlie."

"And there is the odd fact that neither Charlie or Caitlin seem to want any real help at all."

"Right. And yet Charlie really is scared. I've seen fear — and that man has it."

"It doesn't make sense."

Jack didn't respond to that. More deep thoughts churning.

He squinted with one eye. "Mind if I have a wee bit more. Can smell and taste the peat. Great stuff."

"Be my guest. Just remember you're driving through that

mess out there."

"Never forget that. You are right — there is something awfully wrong about all this. But there's this other thing, the brother, Ray."

"His disappearance? Just seems like he left, leaving Charlie in charge—"

"Bingo. That's *it*. I can see a dozen reasons for his leaving. I mean, I vanished from my world and washed up here. But Ray, the good, capable farmer, leaving the place to his incompetent brother? That, I don't get."

Then Sarah had a thought. She knew they were a team, and she also knew there were things in her world that Jack didn't understand, things that could be useful.

"Let me do some digging around about Ray Fox. Maybe check bank records, land titles, all that stuff—"

Jack grinned. "You mean hack around?"

She smiled back. Jack wasn't above bending the rules to do what had to be done.

"Let me worry about the niceties. See what I can find. Might be the 'missing Ray' is nothing—"

Jack killed his second pour.

"Or something. Great idea. And one more thing?"

"Hmm?"

"Whoever did that outside isn't playing around, Sarah. And I am beginning to formulate a plan."

"Plan?"

"More of a trap. Can we meet tomorrow morning, at Tamara's shop? I'll set it up. Say ten-thirty?" Then: "I mean, of course, half past ten."

"Details?"

"Patience, Watson. All will be revealed in the morning. We'll need the help of the all-knowing, most mystical Tamara."

"Really? That massage must have made some impression."

"Don't knock it," he said with a smile. "Did wonders."

"Meanwhile — I'll do some hunting on the net. I can't wait to hear what you're cooking up."

"Me either, actually." He stood up. "Say goodnight to Daniel and Chloe for me."

Then Jack left, and Sarah realised that the house now felt safer simply by his having come over.

And when the rain abated, and she finally went outside, she saw that — before leaving — he had walked around to the back and disposed of the wicker arm and the dead raven for her.

12.

RAY'S SECRET

SARAH LOOKED AT the screen on her MacBook Air, shook her head, and then muttered, "Too wrong."

Grace — sitting at a desk across form her — looked up.

"Wrong? What's 'wrong', Sarah?"

She looked up. She trusted Grace implicitly, considered her as much a confidante as Jack. She could — and would — tell either of them anything.

But hacking into the local bank was not an activity she could share with her assistant.

"Hmm? Oh nothing — just a software glitch."

She looked back at her screen. It had taken just a few minutes to slip through the first line of Greenwood Bank's security. Far too easy — even for an amateur like her.

"How are you getting on?" she said to Grace. "You okay sorting the graphics for the hotel spa weekend?"

"I'm onto it. But did you know that they're planning a Murder Mystery Evening for the weekend, dinner and everything?"

Sarah laughed at that. "Sounds like fun."

"I thought I might go, though I can't see Jeremy sitting through that."

Jeremy, Grace's boyfriend, was a quiet young man who

liked his football.

They seemed to get on well…

"Well, if he says no, count me in," she said, hitting Enter.

And then, after a few navigational tricks, and using the various paths and backdoors that every site has, Sarah was in the main database for the bank.

SARAH LEANED CLOSE.

Still feels wrong, she thought. *Doing it for the right reasons or not.*

From here, she couldn't actually move any funds. *God!* Even this local bank would have sufficient monitoring systems in place to detect that.

But basic, raw information about accounts?

That was a different matter entirely. She could see what any clerk could access after just being hired and a week's training.

She entered 'Ray Fox' into the search bar.

Two accounts popped up, one savings, the other current. Both open to view.

She picked the current account and saw that it had been inactive for the last eighteen months.

Substantial funds in there, which would seem to argue that he eventually planned to come back. And no one — like his brother for example — seemed to be trying to claim those funds.

So far, nothing suspicious. Or useful.

She thought of the Murder Mystery Weekend that Grace had mentioned. Might be fun, once the leaves had begun to fall. *See how the pros really solve crime!*

She decided to check the last transactions before Ray departed. A few bank card purchases. Bills paid. A routine transfer from savings to current account and then — just three weeks before all activity ceased — a big transfer.

Three thousand pounds to Cauldwell & Co, the local estate agents.

She was tempted to share the discovery with Grace, but since this was all illegal, best she gave her PA as much 'plausible deniability' as possible.

She looked up.

"Grace — I'm meeting Jack in an hour, but I've got to dash somewhere beforehand. Back by lunch, swear to God, to dig in with you."

"No worries. Carry on with your sleuthing, boss."

Another smile.

Worth her weight in gold. Discreet and smart.

"Thanks." She headed to the door scooping up a yellow pad.

Could be time to start taking some notes.

CECIL CAULDWELL SAT manning the front desk himself. End of the summer was probably a quiet time for sales and rentals. He looked overdressed for the part, a cream-coloured suit, perfect during midsummer but less so now, with a pale purple tie and matching handkerchief.

The bell over the agency door rang as Sarah breezed in, pad in hand.

"Sarah? Um, how are you?"

Like most of Cherringham, Cecil knew that a visit from Sarah or her American friend these days could mean any number of things.

As Cecil had found out when Mogdon Manor burned

down.

"Cecil, phew! Glad you're here. Just took a chance on it—"

She imagined that if she had called ahead he might have invented some showing he had to do that would — unfortunately, he'd say — have him out of the office.

Surprise can be useful.

He did not, however, offer her a seat.

She had the thought that estate agents are like doctors and undertakers. They know things about people, their families, their money, their lives; things that no one else would know.

"Cecil, I've been helping that young couple out on Mabb's Farm."

"They came to you for help?"

"Not exactly. But other people have, concerned people. And I was just wondering about something…"

Her time with Jack should pay off now. Asking a question when you know the answer. The 'upperhand', as Jack would call it.

"Ray Fox and his sudden departure. Did he ever talk to you at all, perhaps about selling the farm, or—"

"I'm afraid that is client privilege, Sarah. I'm sure you understand."

"Certainly."

Still no offer of a chair was forthcoming.

Cecil was clearly hoping that Sarah would breeze out as quickly as she had breezed in.

"It's just that, well, it appears that Ray did contact you. With him gone and all, I was wondering if you might know something?"

"I don't see what this might have to do with that… couple on the farm. I had nothing to do with *that* arrangement, I can tell you."

Aha…

"But other arrangements you did?"

Cecil shifted in his seat. Now Sarah was glad she was standing. Another little bit of edge.

"Look, it's probably no secret that Ray Fox came to see me."

"And hired you? In some fashion."

Cecil hesitated. And then: "Er, in a way."

"I thought representing a property was free, until the sale that is?"

"Too true, but in this case, he knew that the property could easily, maybe more profitably, be sold in pieces, as lots. That requires discreet evaluations, for machinery, livestock, subdividing the property, the various buildings — even the furniture. Some surveying and proposed plans drawn up. There *is* a fee for that."

"A rather sizeable one?"

Cecil — probably sensing he had already let one cat too many out of the bag — retreated. "I'm afraid that is private. Now if you—"

Sarah made some notes on her pad. Nothing really, but she wanted to have Cecil see her do that and wonder… *what is she writing… what is she thinking… and will this somehow affect me?*

"So, you must have been surprised when Ray just upped and left?"

"Well, naturally because of our conversations I knew he wanted to leave. He was good at running the farm, had built up its value. But he didn't like it. Or the village, for that matter. But he left, as they say, *in media res*. And then to leave everything to that Charlie? *That* I don't understand at all."

"Didn't make sense to you?"

"No. I mean, the property had value - but Ray just walked

away from it. Left it to that stupid — sorry —"

"And that payday, would have been - could still be - good for you."

In the silence that followed Sarah's question, the minute hand from a massive clock in the office produced the loudest click Sarah had ever heard.

Then: "Sarah, the matter is closed for me now. And if you have any more questions, I suggest you go and find Ray Fox. He'll be the one who can answer them — not me."

Sarah smiled.

"I appreciate your help, Cecil."

A 'you're welcome' didn't emerge from the agent's mouth.

She started for the door.

"I'll let you know if we do indeed find Ray Fox and get to ask him some of those same questions."

Again the bell tinkled as she left the office, and she started walking briskly toward the centre of the village, to where Jack would be waiting outside Tamara's shop.

13.

PLANS FOR A GIBBOUS MOON

SARAH SAW JACK standing a few shops down from Moonstones, just in front of the new bookshop, looking at the titles on display. He glanced at the street as Sarah raced across to meet him.

"Am I late?"

"Think you are right on time. You know, I've never read any mysteries like they have in the window here. Interesting, hmm? My line of work and all."

She laughed. "Based on my experience with you — not nearly as interesting as the real thing, I'm sure. Is Tamara expecting us?"

"Yes — but did you find out anything with your wizarding web skills?"

Sarah told Jack about the big payment from Ray, what the money was for, and her visit to Cecil.

"Really? That doesn't make sense. Doesn't add up at all. All that money to prepare for a sale, then no sale?"

"Right. And Jack, you said you were formulating a plan, so how about sharing?"

"I did, didn't I? And it's almost there. Just need to see if we can get Tamara on board and then — soon as we're done with her — I will run it by you, partner."

"Good. I can hardly wait."

"Okay then — let's enter the mystical realm and get this party started."

They walked up to the entrance to Moonstones, and opened the door.

TAMARA WAS WAITING, the lights low in the shop, candles lit everywhere. The air cloyingly thick with incense, the seer dressed in a swirling and ornate turquoise gown.

All Sarah could think — seeing her up close — was *what a character*.

"Jack," Tamara said warmly.

Be careful there, Mr Brennan, Sarah thought, smiling to herself. *The mystic likes what she sees.*

"And you must be Ms Edwards."

What a fortune-teller.

Tamara reached out and took a hand.

"Sarah."

Jack looked around. "Tamara, is there a place where we can sit, in private? Sarah and I have a proposition for you."

Tamara's eyes narrowed, guarded. All this curse stuff could be a boon for her business. Her mystical warmth had suddenly turned to wariness. "Why, yes, in the back."

Then, as an after-thought:

"Let me lock the door. So we won't be disturbed."

And with that done, Sarah and Jack followed Tamara to a small room at the back of the shop.

SARAH GUESSED, FROM the plush red felt covering and its octagonal shape, that this table was probably used for Tarot readings, maybe even… séances.

Did Tamara run séances?

Because if they didn't get some big breaks in this case, they might have to resort to that.

"Okay, tell me what I can do."

Jack looked at Sarah with a glance that implied they were speaking with one voice.

Though Sarah had no idea what he was about to say.

"You see, Tamara, after our conversation the other day, I got to thinking. That poor couple on Mabb's Farm. It's so awful for them. My friend Sarah and I want to do something to help them with their Curse."

Sarah couldn't believe that Jack got that line off without a shred of irony.

"Yes. I understand. Still, the dark forces are not so easily dealt with."

Tamara looked from Jack to Sarah as if she was merely pointing out the obvious. Sarah nodded.

"That's precisely it. You said there were things that might be done?"

Unbelievable, Sarah thought.

She couldn't wait to hear how this would all fit into some kind of plan.

"The Curse, Jack, is ancient. Centuries old. And as you have seen, still alive, still *very* powerful…"

Dramatically, Tamara looked away.

She's got her act down to a tee, Sarah thought. *Very slick.*

Sarah turned to Jack. How far was she going to push this?

And then, matching drama for drama, he looked down. "The poor couple, we just wish we could help somehow…"

Which is when Tamara turned back and took what Sarah guessed those in the healing arts called a 'cleansing breath', and spoke in a low, serious, steady voice.

"There is — perhaps — one thing to be done. There is a rite that can be performed, assuming you have enough gifted ones to form a circle of power."

"And how many would that be?" Sarah asked, the question sounding far too detailed as soon as she'd said it.

"Seven. The rite is as old as those stones. For where there are curses and evil, there are always the good forces of the spirit world. It is not without risk. It can be dangerous."

"I'm sure," Jack said.

Sarah had to wonder: does Tamara really believe that Jack buys all this? Or, in this case, is it all simply a means to an end for the woman?

Which, she assumed, they'd soon get to.

"There are preparations that need be made, and of course the gathering of the others... and—"

Another pause.

"Such a rite, with its attendant risks, those preparations, are not without costs."

Jack smiled. "We, I mean *I*, will pay. I figure," and now he looked at Sarah as if to make sure she wouldn't break character, "We just want to try something, anything to help. Worth a shot, right?"

"Then," Tamara said, "Yes. Something might be attempted. But I cannot promise anything."

Could have guessed that, Sarah thought.

"I understand," Jack replied, equally serious, "So tonight, we can—"

Tamara quickly shook her head.

"No. Not tonight. Jack, Sarah, you can't simply do this on

any night you choose. There really is only one night."

They waited to hear what that perfect night might be.

"And that is the last night of the waxing Gibbous moon, the last night before it turns full. Some call it the Devil's Moon, but it is the Devil and his demons who need fear the power of that moon, that night. Only then, on that night, would our powers be possibly — and I stress *possibly* — strong enough to attempt to end the Curse."

"And that would be…?"

Again, Sarah noted that she was asking another practical question amid this amazing flow of mumbo-jumbo.

And though she was sure that Tamara had the date of every phase of the moon memorised — an occupational necessity, no doubt — the woman opened a leather book, flipped pages on which Sarah could see notes and assorted lunar crescents.

"Luckily not long from now. Just two nights in fact. And," she looked up from her astral booking calendar, "that gives us enough time to prepare."

"Great," Jack said, sounding as if he'd found a restaurant that had his favourite dish on the menu. "Um, can we attend?"

That made Tamara pause.

"Normally, it is just the circle, the seven. But to observe, to stand away…"

She was probably calculating that she didn't want to annoy the client footing the bill for the show.

"Yes. That will be all right. As long as you say and do absolutely *nothing*."

"You got it." Then he leaned close. "And Tamara, I would like this to remain among us and — what did you call the others?"

"The Gifted Ones."

"Yes, Just us. We wouldn't want Caitlin, Charlie spooked

any more. Or the villagers, for that matter."

"My lips are sealed, Jack."

"Good."

"Meet us at the footpath that leads from the road exactly at sunset. It will be dark when we reach Mabb's Circle, dark for the ceremony and the Gibbous moon will be rising."

"If you say so."

Sarah struggled not to laugh aloud at that.

She broke the moment by extending her hand to the mystic.

"We'll see you then."

"Yes. Oh, and as to—"

Jack correctly guessed the end of her sentence. "Right. Just add the costs to my statement for the massage — which was great by the way. I'll fire off a cheque pronto."

A big smile from Tamara, and the two of them stood up, and — the whole thing feeling like a weird mix of the unreal and the absurd — walked out of the shop.

14.

THE PLAN

"You are *too* much," Sarah said when they got out. "I thought I was going to crack up."

He turned to her, his smile broad. "What, not convincing enough?"

She laughed. "I guess it was. Me — it was all I could do not to fall off my chair. So, how about a cup of tea and you tell me the plans for this spell night you set up?"

He shook his head.

"No tea. Don't want anyone to overhear. Least, not what I'm going to tell you."

He pointed across to one of the lanes. "That leads up to the cricket pitch, then down to some fields, right?

"Yes."

"Walk there? And I will talk you through my now fully formulated plan."

"Super…"

THE GRASS WAS still wet from the morning dew, and was long overdue for a cut. But such a rich green. This deep green of the grass, the moss — was something Sarah had missed in the greyness of London.

"Tamara will lead her troupe up there," said Jack. "But I'm also guessing that she and her coven will have a hard time keeping quiet about this most exciting of gigs."

"You want her to talk?"

"Yes, and her pals. Make sure the word gets out. I'll do my part, let it slip down at the pub." A beat. "When Tom's there, Phil Nailor…"

"Wait a second. We've been on that hill. We know what will happen, Charlie will come racing up, shotgun in hand…"

"Bingo."

Sarah paused. She loved this game of figuring out Jack's plan without him telling her. As if he was running some kind of Hogwarts School of Detection.

Which — in a way — it was.

"Hang on. Then… then the farm will be deserted save for Caitlin. If someone knows this is happening, it'll be the perfect time for the dreaded Curse to strike again, right?"

"Hmm, do you live inside my head? Exactly. So, if angry Tom is our guy, he knows he can go there and do something with gun-toting Charlie away. Same with Phil Nailor. Even your Cecil. Though I must admit I have a hard time seeing him dancing across the rooftops with a can of white paint."

"Me too. But you've always said, don't eliminate any suspect until they are, in fact, eliminated. That must go for Tamara as well?"

"Yes. See, if nothing happens, it might indicate that the mystic was responsible. She created the Curse, and poof, she makes it go away. Business should be booming."

Jack looked away, as if re-thinking something.

"And what do we do?" Sarah said.

"We walk with them. But at some point, I'll slip away to watch the farm. You best stay with Tamara to keep Charlie calm when he comes running up to tell them to get off his property."

"Jack — can I say how glad I am that you have absolutely no belief in any curse."

"In my world, people make their own curses. And they fix them too. Either way, should be an interesting and informative evening. Hook baited, and we just wait."

"Knew you'd bring fishing into this."

That gave her another thought.

Sometimes you don't know what you will catch.

Did they have all the possible suspects? And was something else worrying him?

"Any more ideas?"

He stopped and looked away. Then: "I'll be honest. This disappearing Ray thing bothers me. Something wrong there, even though he wanted to leave the farm. Still—"

"We have a trap set."

"Precisely."

She took a breath.

"Right then. I'll make sure I'm all clear for the night, get the kids sorted. But I'd better dash now — I've left Grace with a monster project."

"Go on. And I'll see you at the next Gibbous moon!"

93

15.

THE RING OF STONES

SARAH PARKED IN the muddy layby just off the main road and turned the headlights off. It was late and the road was quiet. Silence settled around them.

"We ready?" she said, turning to Jack.

"Ready as we'll ever be," he replied.

In his winter puffa jacket and black woollen hat Sarah thought he looked like a professional burglar dressed for a profitable night out.

"So, let's go," she said, opening the passenger door.

She locked the car behind them and zipped up her waterproof. Then, checking she had her pencil torch in her pocket, she nodded at Jack and they set off down the long track that led to Mabb's Farm.

They walked in silence at first, both concentrating on the pot-holed track in the darkness, trying to avoid the bigger puddles of black water. Sarah knew that the moon wouldn't be up for at least another hour and for the moment the fields and sloping hill to the side of the track were hardly visible.

It was cold out and the wind was getting stronger. She could just see the dark grey shapes of clouds skidding past in the sky above.

"If anyone drives down here, we'll just have to take our luck in the ditch," said Jack. "Don't want to get caught in the headlights."

"With any luck, Caitlin's left already," she said.

"I hope so," said Jack. "This isn't without its dangers, you know."

Sarah knew that. And she was glad she'd managed to get Ali from the Mother and Toddler group to invite Caitlin and Sammy over for the evening.

If Jack's plan worked then there was going to be some kind of confrontation tonight. And it might be violent.

Not the kind of situation where you'd want a woman and a baby.

Jack put his hand on her arm and gestured ahead. She peered into the gloom and could see movement. Straining her eyes she could just make out figures by the side of the track.

"I guess it's them," she whispered.

Jack shrugged and they both moved on.

Within seconds they'd reached the group — though they didn't exactly look like the witches' coven Sarah had been expecting. Huddled by the fence, in waterproofs and walking gear — and looking thoroughly miserable — were Tamara's Gifted Ones, with various colourful bags at their feet.

Costumes? Brooms?

Sarah nodded to Tamara who introduced her and Jack to the others. They nodded back, but none of them smiled. She didn't recognise any faces.

I guess for a show like this the professionals have to be shipped in, thought Sarah.

"You may walk with us to the circle," said Tamara. "But then you must stay back. The ritual cannot be interrupted. You both understand?"

"Sure," said Jack. "We feel so privileged just to be able to see you at your work."

Sarah nodded in agreement, forcing her face to remain serious.

He's killing me, she thought.

Tamara consulted her watch.

"There is little time," said Tamara. "The moon will rise. We must hasten to the stones!"

"Lead on, Macduff!" said Jack seriously.

Sarah tried hard not to catch his eye. This was not the time to burst out laughing — much as she wanted to.

One by one the Gifted Ones climbed through the barbed wire fence at the side of the track and followed the muddy path across the fields that led up to the woods — and the Ring of Stones.

THE WOOD WAS pitch-black and Sarah seriously doubted they would be able to walk for more than a few yards before losing the track.

Tamara gave permission for torches to be used — but even so, they all huddled close as a group and Sarah noticed that Jack, next to her, seemed just as keen to keep up as she was.

At one point the group stopped and a muttered, whispered discussion took place. Sarah looked around. She could just make out the shape of one or two trees but that was all.

It seemed far colder up here in the woods than it should have been.

"Spooky, huh?" whispered Jack. She knew he wasn't joking.

The wind rustled branches deeper in the dark wood. Instinctively she looked over her shoulder.

Was that a shape? A human — or some animal?

She shivered involuntarily.

"What's happening?" she said to Jack.

"Some kind of rebellion, I think," he whispered back. "Seems one or two of them say there are evil spirits in the wood too. The Gifted Ones are getting spooked."

"No kidding," she said. "I could have told them that for free."

"They don't want to go on."

"Terrific," whispered Sarah. "If they bail, there goes our plan, leaving us stuck up here."

After a few minutes it seemed the argument was over and they all moved ahead again.

But this time Sarah sensed they were going faster — no doubt about it.

And, not a moment too soon, they emerged from the wood onto the open space at the crest of the hill. At a signal from Tamara, the group switched off their torches.

In total darkness now, the stones stood as black shadows — still and ominous. What little light there was played on them and Sarah had to blink to stop them becoming in her imagination frozen figures, stooped men, knights of stone.

The sooner this was over, the better.

But would Charlie see them? Would he come up here?

She watched as the group silently gathered at the edge of the ring and started to pull robes, hats, banners and all sorts of mysterious equipment from their bags.

Tamara came over to her and Jack.

"The moon will rise in thirty minutes," she said.

"What happens now?" said Sarah.

"We will prepare the ring and then the ritual will begin."

"Where do you want us?" said Jack.

"You will stay here," she said. "And you must remain completely quiet. Preferably out of sight. There must be no distractions."

"Will it be dangerous?" said Jack.

"Fear not," said Tamara. "We bring an aura of protection and you are within it because you are with us."

"Phew," said Jack. "That's a relief, Sarah, isn't it?"

"Yes, Jack," said Sarah. "It is."

Too much.

"Tell you what, Tamara," continued Jack, pointing downhill. "We'll just slip down there behind that big boulder and you'll hardly notice we're here."

Tamara nodded.

"When the moon has risen and its beams strike the stones, then the cleansing shall begin."

Then she turned and went back to join her fellow-exorcists.

Jack turned to Sarah.

"Wish I could stay up here and watch," said Jack. "I'm sure this will have to be seen to be believed."

"Hmm," said Sarah. "I've literally got a ring-side seat."

"I'll text you if I see Charlie," said Jack. "Of course, he could be up here already. The light from those torches might have been visible from the farm."

"If he didn't see the torches," said Sarah, "he'll see those for sure..."

And she pointed to Tamara and the others who were now planting a great ring of oil-flares around the stone circle.

"I'm heading off," said Jack. "When they set fire to those things, the whole hillside's going to light up like day. *That* he's got to see."

"Be careful," said Sarah. Suddenly this all seemed very real.

And very dangerous.

"Piece of cake," said Jack with a wink, turning and heading downhill at a crouch.

And then he was gone.

16.

THE MOON RISES

JACK EDGED HIS way along the side of the old milking shed, taking care to stay in the shadows. From inside the barn he could just hear the noise of cattle — restless, nudging their stalls.

A floodlight blazed across the courtyard between the barns — Charlie had clearly decided to invest in decent security since his troubles begun.

The other day when Jack had been up on the hill, he'd memorised the layout of the farm. He knew that the farmhouse itself was on the other side of the next barn. He had no choice — he was going to have to make a run for it across the muddy yard and just hope that Charlie wasn't still out on the farm somewhere working.

Or that whoever they were trying to lure into the farm to do their worst tonight hadn't already arrived — maybe under cover like he was.

Hiding somewhere in one of the barns, or in a hedgerow or a ditch. Waiting...

But Jack knew he had no choice. It was now, or never.

He ran fast and low — nearly slipped in all the cow mess — but reached the cover of the hay barn without hearing the bang of a shotgun.

Stage one, complete.

Now for the really tricky part — finding Charlie without Charlie finding him.

But as he rounded the barn in the darkness and at last got a good view of the farmhouse itself, he could see that his luck was holding.

The lights in the house were on — and the curtains were all open.

And in the sitting room at the front of the house, a familiar figure was moving back and forth. Jack crept across the last twenty yards of concrete yard until he was just to one side of the window. Slowly, he stood up and pressed himself against the Cotswold stone of the farmhouse, his back creaking.

Jeez, if I'm going to be doing more of this I need to get back in shape.

Used to hit the gym at One Police Plaza nearly every day.

Gotten a little lazy in the village…

He edged closer to the side of the window, then turned his head to look in properly.

The room was sparsely furnished. Sofa, armchairs — and a big log-burner ablaze. Charlie stood, his back to the window, a glass in one hand. Jack could see that the farmer was talking — but the room was empty.

Jack scanned the rest of the room: various children's toys and a buggy were piled up in one corner; an old farmhouse table and chairs stood in front of the window.

A bottle of cheap whiskey sat on the table, half empty and the screw-top nowhere to be seen.

Jack pulled back as Charlie suddenly spun round and walked straight toward the table and the window. Even through the glass, Jack could hear him muttering, then the slam of the bottle on the table as he finished pouring himself a refill.

Charlie's getting a bit wired…

Jack looked at his old service watch with the big hands and the luminous dial. The moon would be rising right now though with the heavy cloud it might be some minutes before its effect would be seen.

Then, as if on some kind of ethereal cue, he saw flames flicker into life up on top of the hill. One by one, the ritual flares girding the stone circle ignited — and just as he'd hoped, they were starkly visible from down here on the farm.

From inside the farm, there was the sound of smashing glass and a loud scraping of furniture.

He knew what the sound meant: Charlie had seen the flames through the window.

Jack crawled under the window to the corner of the building where a small hedge provided some cover, and then he squatted down in the darkness.

Sure enough, the front door burst open and Charlie emerged, his shotgun over his arm. Jack watched as the farmer marched over to one of the barns, cursing loudly to himself.

There was the sound of an engine starting and headlights pierced the darkness in front of the barn, then Charlie emerged on the back of a four-wheel ATV, the engine loud in the enclosed yard.

Jack pulled back deeper into the shadow of the hedge as the twin beams flashed across the front of the house.

And then Charlie was gone, along the track towards the field which led up the hill to the stones.

Silence.

Jack took out his phone and sent a text.

'Charlie on his way. He's had a few. Be careful. Anything bad looks like it will happen — let me know.'

Then he settled down to wait. For the real work of the night was still to come.

SARAH HAD BEEN sitting on the grass with her back against a boulder, watching Tamara and the others prepare the ritual.

First they'd changed into their white robes. Then they'd sprinkled salt between the stones, set fire to some Ash leaves and laid out banners with symbols she didn't recognise. Every now and then there'd been a disagreement in the group about some detail.

I guess the handbook for these ancient rituals is still being written, she thought.

Then Tamara had planted five candles in the centre of the circle and ceremoniously drew white lines between them making a pentacle shape.

And finally a chief witch or warlock of some kind — a bedraggled looking young guy with long, dank hair — flicked a zippo at each of the oil flares and the whole place had lit up.

This had been the signal for the seven Gifted Ones to enter the Circle and start chanting, the smoke from the flares swirling dramatically around them.

If she hadn't had a risky confrontation with a half-crazed farmer to look out for, she would have quite enjoyed this.

It's just like one of those beach shows we used to take the kids to on holiday in the Far East, she thought.

But Jack's text had reminded her to be watchful, especially as Charlie had been drinking.

She edged around to the side of the rock which faced the hillside and the farm below, so that now her back was to the magic ritual and the flares.

From here she could already see the lights of Charlie's

vehicle heading away from the farm, far below.

And she could also see the ominous shape of the white, glowing Gibbous moon now rising over Cherringham. Still low in the sky, it looked enormous, threatening.

A hint of what was to come…

JACK WAS FEELING nervous. He'd known all along that timing was everything for this plan to work. The lights up at the stones would lure Charlie away.

And with luck, whoever had been attacking the farm would now turn up and have another go. But it all depended on whether the gossip machine had done its work.

Though Charlie had been gone a good ten minutes the farm was still eerily silent.

Sometimes, plans don't work, Jack knew.

Motionless, he strained his ears into the night, alert for the slightest sound.

Luckily the darkness was lifting. The moon had surfaced above the farmhouse, shedding just enough light to make the faintest of shadows across the concrete yard.

Up above, Jack could now see clouds, rolling past on the wind.

Here in the corner of the farmhouse and the hedge though, Jack knew he was still invisible. He just needed to wait patiently and—

From the far barn came a metallic — *clang*.

Not a sound made by restless cattle. No — that was a sound made by a human…

Another *clang*.

And then a figure appeared at the corner of the barn,

walking awkwardly. Medium height, in a black hoodie and jeans, face obscured. Even in the moonlight, hard to identify at this distance — maybe thirty yards.

Then Jack understood why the person's walk was so uneven.

The intruder was lugging a large jerry-can — and had begun pouring fluid from it along the side of the barn.

The smell was strong and instant — *gasoline*.

And Jack felt a rush of adrenaline go through his body. This amount of fuel — the place would go up like a bomb.

The figure had stopped, put down the can and was rooting around searching pockets...

Jack knew instantly what they were looking for. Matches — or a lighter.

He needed to act.

Had to stop them now.

He got up from his crouched position and started to run, both knees sending up a sharp spike of pain.

And as he ran, he saw almost in slow motion the figure now just yards ahead of him strike a match... then clumsily drop it into the mud. Then the figure took out another—

—and just before the match sparked Jack had crossed the yard and hit hard like a linebacker, his shoulder catching the person in the small of the back.

Oof! That hurt...

His tackle sent both of them crashing to the muddy concrete together, matches spilling, legs flailing, bodies hitting the hard ground, Jack's hands ripping at the hoodie and pulling it back, and the intruder's face suddenly visible and Jack saying — in shock and total surprise—

"*You?*"

17.

THE CURSE REVEALED

SARAH HAD STEPPED into playground fights when kids' tempers got out of control but this little fracas was off the dial.

She watched the coven's conflict unfold with a mixture of horror and amusement.

Charlie had leaped off his four-wheel and grabbed hold of one of the flaming torches. He was now waving it around like some kind of medieval warrior — a drunken warrior.

As he roamed the circle of stones in a fury, the Gifted Ones started alternately shouting and hurling handfuls of salt at him.

Not the demon they'd expected...

In the middle of the circle, Tamara remained tranquil, ignoring Charlie, bravely trying to finish the "un-cursing".

"Spirits of the Stones! I command you — relinquish your hold!" she repeated to the corners of the circle, occasionally ducking as Charlie's fiery brand swept over her head.

She's keeping her cool. I've got to say that for her, Sarah thought.

Sarah meanwhile kept firm hold of the shotgun which luckily Charlie had dropped when he slipped in the mud during his first angry attack.

With the practised ease of an army brat, she'd broken the gun and ejected the cartridges.

"You crazy lot — get the hell off my land with all this crap!" shouted Charlie, hurling a flare at the weedy warlock with the long hair when he poked his head round a stone.

This is actually comical. Definitely ready for YouTube, Sarah thought.

"There is evil here, Charlie Fox, and you cannot deny it!" shouted Tamara. "The souls of the cursed cry out for release!"

"No! No!" wailed Charlie. "That's a load of—" another swing of the torch, "Bollocks!"

Sarah could see now that Charlie was losing it, his eyes wild and his arms flailing. It wasn't just the drink — she suddenly realised. Something else... This was a man close to breaking point.

She didn't hear Jack arriving from behind. But he came not a minute too soon, his hand on her shoulder as he passed by her and walked straight towards the circle.

"Charlie," he said gently. Jack must have talked to so many men also at the end of their tether. Again: "Charlie," his voice not loud but still cutting through the mayhem.

Sarah saw Charlie turn now, confused by yet another unexpected arrival.

"You?" he said, wiping his eyes with his forearm. "God! What are you doing here?"

"Like we said the first time, Charlie. Here to help."

"Nothing helps. Nothing can help."

Sarah watched as Jack approached him carefully.

"I think this will. Or at least it might help you understand what's been happening."

He looked around at Tamara and her group, now frozen, watching Jack.

Then she watched as Jack turned back and called down the hill.

"Come on," he said, as if he was speaking to a spooked animal. "It's okay."

And Sarah watched as a hooded figure appeared out of the darkness and trudged up the hill towards them, head bowed. At first she didn't recognise who it was — but Charlie was quicker.

"Caitlin?"

Caitlin walked into the pool of light from the still-burning flares, and pulled back her hoodie. Sarah could see she was covered in mud, her hair matted, her face streaked.

"What's happened, love?" said Charlie. Then, anxiously, "Where's Sammy? Where is he?"

"He's all right, Charlie. Don't worry," said Caitlin. "He's with Ali in the village. Asleep probably by now. If she's lucky."

"B-but what are you doing here Cait?" said Charlie. "You'll catch your death."

Sarah looked at Jack. This didn't make sense. What was happening?

Jack nodded at her. She could see his jacket was covered in dirt, too.

Caitlin came further up the hill until she was standing just a yard from Charlie.

"It was me, Charlie."

"What do you mean, love? I don't—"

But instantly Sarah knew what Caitlin was saying.

"It was *me*," Caitlin repeated. "I'm the one who did all those things. The fire. The footprints on the roof."

Sarah saw Charlie shake his head. This didn't compute...

"No," he said. "It's other people. Tom, I reckon — or one of them other bastard farmers. Or this lot, taking advantage—"

"No, Charlie," Caitlin said firmly. "I'm telling you. It was me."

"But why?" said Charlie. "That doesn't make sense."

"I wanted to leave. Go back to the flat. Back to how it used to be. We were happy there. Remember?"

"You should have… could have told me."

"You didn't listen. Wouldn't listen."

"So you burned the farm?"

"You changed, Charlie. Minute we moved here. You turned… bad. Horrible. This place. The Curse,"

"She's right, Charlie," said Tamara. "It's the Curse!"

Sarah had forgotten Tamara and the Gifted Ones: she could see them now huddled together at the stones with their burning flares, looking just like a Greek chorus.

"No, Tamara," said Jack. "There's no Curse — is there, Charlie?"

Charlie turned to Jack, then back to Caitlin.

"I thought — if the farm makes you unhappy," continued Caitlin. "I could get rid of the farm. Then we could just leave."

"It's not as simple as that, love," said Charlie.

"Because it's not about the farm," said Jack. "It's about your brother, isn't it?"

Now it was Sarah's turn to be surprised. Jack often kept his thoughts and cards close.

Like now…

"What do you mean?" said Caitlin. Then, turning to Charlie, "What does he mean?"

"It's about Ray," said Jack. "Isn't it?"

Again, Sarah saw Charlie turn and peer at Jack as if it were Jack who was now haunting him.

"Ray," said Charlie, almost to himself. "My brother. Yes, it is about Ray."

"So let Ray look after the place," said Caitlin — as confused as Sarah was. "His farm. He buggered off. If the place needs looking after, he can come back and—"

"He can't though, can he, Charlie?" said Jack.

Jack's figured something out, thought Sarah.

The contract with Cauldwell & Co; Ray vanishing; Charlie changing, becoming different.

But what?

"No, he can't," said Charlie. Charlie lowered his torch as if defeated. "He can't… because he's dead."

Sarah heard a sudden intake of breath, in unison, from the Greek Chorus.

She watched as Charlie took a breath himself and his arms dropped at his side.

"And I killed him. It was my fault."

With the flames from the torches swirling behind him, the robed figures lined up before the stones, his wife standing alone in front of him and Jack Brennan at his side…

Charlie Fox finally told his story.

And Sarah felt that they were all somehow taking part in a Stone Age ritual, all participants in an ancient court set within the stone circle that had not been convened for thousands of years — but nevertheless still had powers of justice.

18.

LOOSE ENDS

"THAT IS JUST awesome," said Daniel, somehow managing to walk backwards up the steep track without falling over or bumping into Riley who was threading circles around their feet.

"The power of forensic science," said Jack without breaking step.

He'd made a promise to himself not to stop until they reached the summit — no matter how much his legs complained.

If Sarah and the kids can do it, I'm damned if I can't, he thought.

And as if to prove a point Chloe made a break for the top.

"Last one there's a—"

"Hey!" said Daniel. "Not fair!"

Jack watched Daniel turn and race after her.

"He'll be lucky," said Sarah, next to him. "She won the four hundred metres this summer and he's been skipping football training."

"Just don't you try it on me," said Jack.

"You kidding?" said Sarah. "I thought I was the one lagging behind."

"I'm just a better actor," said Jack.

Head down, Jack carried on up the track, matching Sarah's

confident stride. After all, it had been his idea to come up here on this clear, sunny afternoon.

And Sarah's idea to bring a hot lunch with them in a backpack as a reward.

The flat-topped escarpment with its Neolithic ditches was about six miles east of Cherringham and Jack had been promising himself the climb since he'd moved to England.

Recent events had given it extra meaning, he had realised.

"You think it's pretty certain that the three bodies the police found are the witches?" said Sarah, interrupting his thoughts.

"From what I hear," said Jack. "The clothing, the marking on the necks. The way they were laid out — a ritual burial from hundreds of years ago."

"So, all along they were up there in the woods, by the stones," said Sarah. "No wonder we all felt spooky going through there. Then with Ray too…"

"Woods are cold. Woods are dark. People shiver."

"Oh yeah," said Sarah, grinning. "I know you were spooked just like me, Jack."

Jack had to laugh.

"Maybe. If I was — you better keep that to yourself."

They reached the top. Ahead the grass levelled out. Riley was chasing Daniel round and round in circles, barking madly. Chloe was leaning back on a bench, eyes shut in the weak autumn sun.

Jack turned — and there was the view he'd been looking forward to.

Below them in the valley the Thames looped and turned gently, bright against the sunlight. Jack could see his barge on its mooring. And across the river, he could see Cherringham slumbering through another Sunday afternoon, shops shut, pubs quiet.

"See the stones?" said Sarah next to him.

He shaded his eyes. On a wooded hill beyond Cherringham the stone circle above Mabb's Farm stood out, the sunlight catching the grey slabs.

"You believe Charlie's story?" she said.

"Sure, why not?" Jack answered. "I can believe he and his brother had a fight. Ray tells him he's selling up — Charlie, always passed over, loses control. And we've both seen Charlie lose control. Ray goes down — wallop — hits his head on the fireplace. The pathologist can confirm that part. Then — with his brother dead — Charlie panics."

"But why not just go to the police, own up? If it was an accident."

"You see — that's *it*. He'd never get the farm, that way," said Jack. "No, Charlie had wanted that place since he was a lad, ever since his dad preferred his brother over him. Lucky Ray — Unlucky Charlie. Imagine living with that? It had been an accident — but it was also a chance for him."

"So he just digs a hole in the woods, dumps his brother in and forgets all about him," said Sarah.

"That's the trouble," said Jack. "He couldn't forget. Could you? Whole thing was eating him up."

"And the Curse... became real."

"Exactly."

"What about Caitlin? You think she really didn't know?"

Jack considered this.

"Not consciously," said Jack. "Least, I don't think so. She just wanted help, wanted her old life back, her old Charlie — unlucky or not."

"Pretty dramatic way of getting it."

"It worked though, didn't it?" said Jack. "Charlie won't be charged with murder. It'll be manslaughter. Maybe a couple of other charges. But I'd bet he'll be out in less than five. Maybe half that.

"And Caitlin?"

"No-one's going to prosecute her for setting fire to her own property. And the Wicker Man stunt in your garden…?"

Sarah shook her head.

"They'll be back in the flat together — as a family," said Jack.

"Unlucky Charlie goes back to being Happy-Go-Lucky Charlie."

"Winners all round," said Jack.

"Except for Tamara," said Sarah. "No more curses to keep the shop going."

"Oh, I'm not so sure about that," said Jack. "She and her Gifted Ones were pretty damned sure there was something bad going down in the woods."

"You're right. The souls of the witches…"

"Yep," said Jack. "I've also been putting the word around how great her massages are," he said grinning. "Can't see her being out of business any time soon."

"You're all heart, Jack," said Sarah.

"You know — I guess I am," said Jack, propping his backpack against the bench next to Chloe. "Now, where's that hot chilli and rice you promised me?"

He watched as Sarah started to unpack the food. Then she turned:

"Not just chilli," said Sarah, taking a bottle out of her backpack. "Iced Bud, too."

"You're kidding me?"

He took the bottle, opened it, and drank a mouthful. Then he sat down and leaned against his pack.

"How about that," said Jack, breathing in deep and taking

in the view. "That tastes so good."

And not for the first time, he thought: *This is the life.*

NEXT IN THE SERIES:

CHERRINGHAM
A COSY CRIME SERIES

THE BODY IN THE LAKE

Matthew Costello & Neil Richards

Cherringham parish council has invited Laurent Bourdain, mayor of a French village on the Brittany coast, to a gala reception to join the two villages in a mutually beneficial 'twinning'. The venue: Lady Repton's manor house, which her grandson hopes to turn into a world-class conference center.

An elaborate dinner worthy of the French dignitary has been prepared. But as the night wears on, and the wine flows, the mayor will vanish from the celebration, only to be found floating dead in the nearby lake.

An accident it would appear, until Jack and Sarah start to piece together what really happened to the body in the lake.

ABOUT THE AUTHORS

Matthew Costello (US-based) and **Neil Richards** (UK) have been writing TV scripts together for more than twenty years. The best-selling Cherringham series is their first collaboration as fiction writers: since its first publication as ebooks and audiobooks the series has sold over a million copies.

Matthew is the author of many successful novels, including *Vacation* (2011), *Home* (2014) and *Beneath Still Waters* (1989), which was adapted by Lionsgate as a major motion picture. He has written for The Disney Channel, BBC, SyFy and has also written dozens of bestselling games including the critically acclaimed *The 7th Guest*, *Doom 3*, *Rage* and *Pirates of the Caribbean*.

Neil has worked as a producer and writer in TV and film, creating scripts for BBC, Disney, and Channel 4, and earning numerous Bafta nominations along the way. He's also written script and story for over 20 video games including *The Da Vinci Code* and *Broken Sword*.

CPSIA information can be obtained
at www.ICGtesting.com
Printed in the USA
LVHW040911171220
674417LV00007B/1076